Chapter One: E

They say fear darkness
It's where light is missed
But aren't shadows proof
That something exists?
Sometimes to appreciate the good
We have to see what is not right
Without acknowledging the shadows
How can we ever truly welcome the light?

People that don't feel loved enough often do strange things. Such as paying attention to ensure that no one else suffers the same way. Caring one-sidedly. Protecting people without being asked. Particularly those that have an outstanding or redeeming quality. One that makes them even less deserving of the aforementioned hell.

Vix didn't have to look into his eyes to know that Tiro had a beautiful soul.

Besides, that would have required eye contact and Vix knew she was several lifetimes away from making such a profound connection with someone like him. However, knowing that failed to stop her from following him, as he apparently gave up on waiting for wheels and decided to use his feet in-

1

stead. A very inconvenient choice, since the mere thought of sharing the same space as him beneath the shelter of the bus stop was enough to make her trip over her *own* two feet. Unlike her, Tiro moved like an angel. Graceful, musical. But, at the same time, like a baby animal. Clumsy, quietly fizzing with unspent sparks.

At the edge of her peripheral vision, Tiro replaced his phone in his pocket and adjusted the earphone that was already curled into his ear, the second one hanging down to rest on the front of his dark ochre coat. Normally, she hated that colour. Today, it complimented the loose white shirt beneath it and the golden cream skin beneath that ...

What the -? Her brows lowered before he turned and started walking down the road, away from where she was standing. *Where's* **he** *going?*

Only moments ago, he had been looking at his phone, lifting his head to scan the street rolling away from them, its length decorated by dangling skeletons, exaggerated masks, and cobwebs that had been awaiting this exact night for the better part of a month. She had scratched the side of her face, locking eyes with a luminous, grinning pumpkin across the road, her nails scraping the rim of her glasses as his gaze had swung her way.

Too fast, she had berated herself, *slow down or he'll see.*

He was very good at seeing things and then pretending like he hadn't. People stumbling over waste paper bins, hastily catching things that they had just knocked over, a cup of juice that had missed a pair of lips parted in a dazed grin. He would turn his face away from the person, sweeping stray strands of

Don't Disappoint Me: Volume One

Don't Disappoint Me, Volume 1

Sakinah Baksh

Published by Sakinah B, 2019.

This is a work of fiction. Similarities to real people, places, or events are entirely coincidental.

DON'T DISAPPOINT ME: VOLUME ONE

First edition. December 15, 2019.

Written by Sakinah Baksh.

For my family ...

Using the collective term so that no one can accuse me
of favouritism.

downy black hair behind one ear as he did so, a smile tilting the naturally downward curve of his mouth.

As her eyes followed him, Vix's hand drifted down to clench the side of her khaki jacket, the padded interior between her fingers soothing the inflamed feelings that she kept away from her features. During those moments, she usually saw what Tiro hadn't. Most of those accidents had happened because those people had been staring at him. But that was okay. There was no need for him to feel responsible for the effect he unconsciously had on the world.

He slipped his palms into his trouser pockets, shoulders hunching ever so slightly, seconds away from hugging himself. Vix craned her neck as she shuffled away from the bus stop, the tell-tale glare of headlights missing from the dim length of tarmac. She was only supposed to follow him to the bus stop today. That was the promise she had made to herself ten minutes ago as she left their work place, several long strides behind him. Once he got on the bus, he would be in a public space. After that, it was a five minute walk to his front door. She had known that knowledge would come in handy one day. It had almost been handy ... until he had decided to wander the streets on the only night that creeps felt that they were entitled to unleash their freakiness on the rest of society.

Creeps like you? Vix swallowed the guilty question, focusing on the facts. *If he goes this way, he'll have to pass at least three pubs ... and then there's that side road. Why tonight of all nights, damn it?!*

Pulling her dark grey beanie down a little lower over furrowed eyebrows, she stuck to the shadows of his trail into the deceptively sweet, chocolate-scented night. The cold seemed to cling to his posture, more intense than usual without the excess fabric of his shirt flapping it away.

He's not even wearing his autumn coat. She rubbed the tip of her index finger across the smooth width of her thumbnail repeatedly, chewing her lower lip as though it were an idea. *It'll take him at least twenty minutes to get home this way. Why didn't he wait for the bus?*

Theories popped up into the focal point of her mind's eye, random rather than systematic. He hadn't been sneaking glances at his phone or visiting the toilets more than usual. It wasn't his birthday. He hadn't made any calls during lunch nor agreed to any after work plans, despite everything the women in the canteen had said at lunch. He had left the building before anyone could even attempt to kidnap him for the night, sliding out of his desk a few seconds earlier than he was supposed to, knowing that nobody would dream of paying any attention to his daily misconduct. He probably assumed that he was only allowed to get away with it because he worked a few minutes overtime just as often. Despite his early departures, this was the first time he had seemed in a hurry to get back home.

Maybe it's a pre-arranged date. The thought struck her like the memory of being punched in the chest, knocking her back a step in some distant place. *He could've arranged it last night. Maybe he's got someone waiting at home for him ...*

She had already had this conversation with herself, perhaps a month or so after his existence had blessed the stagnant stretch of her life. One day, he would find someone for himself. And that was okay, regardless of whether she thought that person was worthy of him or not. It didn't matter because – with or without anyone else in the picture – there was no way she would ever be anything more than a colleague to him. That description alone was spreading the truth thinner than she liked.

In front of her, Tiro gave in to the urge of the weather, rubbing his upper arms and groaning shakily. The silence of the evening only amplified the contrast between his delicate features and the abyss of his voice. It was the quality that usually drew attention in the first place. His heavenly visage often sealed the deal. A car approached from the opposite direction, illuminating the rounded angles of his silhouette, the soft curls at the ends of his black hair, the length of his legs visible beneath a suede coat that just wasn't warm enough. Not for the first time – and most certainly not for the last – Vix felt the air catch somewhere between her lungs and voice box, halted by the sheer eloquence of his appearance. Tiro exhaled out warm carbon dioxide, breath billowing out on either side of him like cigarette smoke.

No closer than this. Vix inhaled deeply as she passed through the patch of his diffusing breath. A faint sweetness lingered in the air but that could have belonged to the pumpkins silently cooking from the inside out. *I promise.*

She still couldn't decide whether she preferred the less engaged Tiro, who seemed lost in another world with the ghost of a previous expression hovering over his face like a hologram. Or the one that owned the centre of attention stage, who raised authentically slanted brows and opened his mouth in an encouraging half smile whoever had been lucky enough to snare him in a conversation. He seemed to disregard qualities, such as age, sex and race, as a personal rule. As though he were the equal opportunities act incarnate.

He turned into a side road and she quickened her pace, moving as soundlessly as her grey trainers would allow.

Not that it matters. She eyed the pub that they were about to pass, the rumble of voices blending with the pulse of music in a distinctly headache inducing hum. Tiro swerved off to the side, keeping on the furthest side of the path. *Is it the noise that bothers him this much? Or the smell? Maybe its all the possibilities that put him on edge. Oh wait, I forgot. He's not me –*

"Hey Kaelyn!" yelled someone standing outside the pub, hurrying over to where Tiro reluctantly slowed to a stop.

"Why do you keep calling me that?" he said, laughter masking the way he almost ducked away from the arm that the stranger slung around his shoulders.

Vix stopped, looking down at her phone without turning the screen on, muffled fury whiting out her vision for a second.

"I knew it'd make you stop," said the man, his spiky hair nearly brushing the side of Tiro's face. "How many guys do you know called Kaelyn?"

"How many guys do you know called Tiro?" He sounded like he was smiling but she had seen his face after being addressed by his surname, statue-like in its muted severity.

Why do people insist on being so freakin' insensitive? Vix put her phone away so she wouldn't throw it, falling in line behind them as Tiro began walking again. *What do they get out of it?*

"True, true. But I like it." The stranger was actually Rob, a senior adviser who worked in a different department but often had to visit their side of the building for information. He usually made a bee-line straight for Tiro's desk, unless the younger adviser wasn't sitting at it.

"You're welcome to it," replied Tiro, sarcasm masked as sincerity dripping from his tone. "Should we swap?"

"As much as I'd love to take you up on that offer, I think it suits *you* better," chuckled Rob, his arm tightening around Tiro's neck, swinging him around until they were both facing the pub. "That aside, how about you come join us? Everybody else dressed up."

Vix side stepped hastily and slowed down, swallowing hard as their line of sight missed her by inches. Standing outside the pub, a skeleton, a witch and something that looked like a spider-zombie hybrid waved back as Rob pointed them out. Tiro's widened eyes became sparkling slits as he grinned, still partially head-locked by Rob, and raised a hand to acknowledge them.

"As much as I'd love to take you up on that offer, I'm afraid I can't tonight." He pulled Rob's arm away from his throat and straightened up, nose scrunched up into an apology. "I've got plans."

"Really? Going on a spooky date?" Their colleague continued walking with him and Vix hissed under her breath as their voices dropped out of ear shot.

Thankfully, Tiro gave her the answer she had been seeking since they had left work, raising a hand and shaking his head emphatically. An awkward shrug raised his shoulders.

So he's not going on a date? She passed Rob's friends without looking at them, holding her breath and controlling her pace until all three of them and the scent of bad grapes were a good distance behind her. *He should've just lied. This idiot isn't getting the hint any time soon.*

Up ahead, Tiro turned a corner and waved, his smile strained when Rob continued to follow him despite the obvious parting movement of his hand. She caught a glimpse of the potent grin on Rob's face before they both disappeared from view and her stomach twinged darkly, forebodingly. The scrape of her own footsteps was too loud for comfort, echoing in the calm before what seemed to be an impending storm.

Who cares if he hears me. She reached the corner, pausing to peer around it. *As long as he's okay, I don't care what –*

Rob's arm had somehow found its way around Tiro's waist, his touch sickeningly over familiar for a friend or relative, let alone for a fellow member of staff. He had the same awful grin on his face as the younger man twisted around to face him. She couldn't hear but his lips formed unmistakably persuasive words, reaching out with his other hand. Tiro pushed his arms away and stepped back, searching his features. A faint smile trembled on his face despite the confusion in his eyes. As if he could still pass off Rob's advances as a joke.

I'm going to kill him. Vix ignored the jolt in her gut, stepping out from behind the corner and onto the secluded side road lit by flickering street lamps. Rob grabbed Tiro by the wrist, wicked laughter on his face, and pulled the other man closer. Something growled viciously at the back of her mind. *I swear I'm gonna murder –*

Rob bent his head, maybe to whisper the words "Gotcha" in Tiro's ear, maybe to do something less forgivable.

Vix never found out.

Someone grunted, half surprise, half discomfort, louder than the pulse in her ears. She had a split second to identify the voice as Rob's rather than Tiro's before the younger man took half a step back, yanking something out of their colleague's stomach. The older man pressed a hand to his gut. It was too dark to see exactly what had happened yet something about his posture gave everything away. The pained disbelief on the side of his face was somehow familiar yet totally alien to her eyes.

Wh – What? Vix froze mid-step, stumbling over her own shock, the oxygen in her veins turning to fog. *That's a –*

The small blade spun in Tiro's hand as he raised it over his head and plunged it back down, this time into Rob's chest. Again and again, despite their colleague's arms, raised in self-defence. Despite the fact that he was choking on something that may have been words but were now too clogged with blood to identify. The panic that had layered Tiro's behaviour seconds ago melted away into cold composure, fitting him like tailored clothes, the thin fingers of his other hand shackling Rob's elbow.

No – Vix opened her mouth but language failed her just like many things in life, her raised hand stilled by the impossibility of what she was seeing. *No, that can't – He **can't** –*

Rob's body spasmed like a creepy puppet under the frenzied yet rhythmic rise and fall of Tiro's hand, oddly out of place on a night that should have welcomed it. Silence roared in her head but Vix was silent as the attacker- turned-victim collapsed, first to his knees before toppling sideways. He lay there, jerking as if he could still feel the knife. One arm blindly roved the ground beside him, his body curled up as if he were suddenly feeling the chill of the evening. Perhaps he was, the heat leaking from his body through all the holes that Tiro had just punched into him.

He did that. The fluid in her eyes felt just as frozen. *He did that to Rob ...*

Tiro kicked aside Rob's reaching hand casually, as if it were a stray football, before crouching down next to him. His hair fell forward, covering his eyes but not the movement of his perfect lips, shaping words that were fuzzy in the aftermath of all she had just witnessed. He wiped his weapon clean on Rob's jacket as though sponging jam off a butter knife and stood up, stashing away the deadly length of metal too fast to work out where. Taking a few steps back, he held his arms out in front of him and turned his palms over as if making sure they were clean.

The street lamp above him decided to stop flickering for a few seconds, illuminating the slight heave of his chest, the victorious quirk of his mouth and the blood spotting the flawless skin of his face and throat. He looked like someone that had been cast from heaven; in the middle of taking his anger out on the earth he had been banished to. Someone who had realised all too soon that maybe earth met their needs better. He lifted a hand, smearing red marks across his jaw in an attempt to rub them off before glancing down at his stained fingertips.

And then sideways, directly at her, his head turning slowly a few seconds later to follow his gaze.

Oh – Her thoughts turned to scribble, a mass of lines that had once made sense. The fog in her veins turned to steel. *Sh –*

The tang of old coins mixed with the sourness of public bathrooms. And her urge to run overpowered a violent need to throw up. Everything pulsated around her, within her, as she ran. Unable to remember her decision to move.

Tiro just stabbed Rob. Cold air trailed through her short hair and down her spine like water, paying no attention to the padded jacket that had warded it off this whole time. *Rob's dying back there.*

Street lamps were blazing suns in the dark desert above, blurred beyond the water veiling her eyes. Her heart beat frantically in her ears, urging her to move faster. Against the dead weight of her muscles. Against the inexperience of her joints. Drowning out all thoughts except one.

If I don't get away now ... I never will.

She had no memory of passing the pub. Or reaching the bus station. The block of offices where she worked reared up before her and Vix finally slowed, gasping hard enough to vomit, clutching at the front of her clothes and pulling them. As if doing so would lure air into her brain.

Where is he? She came up against the front door, locked for the day. Stared through reinforced panes into its unlit interior. Unable to turn around for answers. *Did he follow me? Have I lost him?*

Her shaking palms left smudges of steam on the glass surface. Her reflection bloomed into view, eyes wide behind her glasses. Mouthing words that she had never learnt how to say out loud. Words she was even less likely to scream into the twilight.

What do I do ... What do I do? Her own face offered no reassurance, drained of colour, of solutions. *Tiro is ... Tiro just ...*

The memory of his face as he stabbed Rob in the chest popped up before her. His features had still managed to look perfect, despite being warped into a delighted snarl. Bile rose up in her throat, coating her tongue with acid. It filled her lungs, tried to burn away the obsession that her brain could not digest on its own. It was difficult to breathe, think, see the face in the glass next to her own –

Vix let out a strangled cry as she whirled around, too slow to stop Tiro's cool fingers from clamping down upon her throat, crushing her against the door. His spearmint-sharp breath washed over her heated face, flooding her already sluggish thoughts. Competing with the bile in her wind pipe, the thud of her heart in her ears and the tears that had finally broken free from her eyes. Her lungs were caving in. She gripped frantically at his sleeves to ease the pressure against her throat and everything was going up icy flames.

Tiro knew she existed. Tiro was touching her. Tiro had just killed someone.

Tiro ... was killing her.

Mercilessly. Without a trace of hesitation on his face.

Willing to end her life without caring who she was or who she would ever be.

This can't be happening. Indignation welled up inside her along with the fear of embracing something that she had desired for as long as she could remember. *I can't let this happen.*

With a determined whimper, Vix kicked out at him, her shoe grazing the side of his shin before she used it to push off from the door behind her. For a second, she managed to twist out of his grip and force him back a step. Coughing wetly as she tried to steal a lungful of oxygen and dared to hope that she could fight him off.

A moment later, as if he had given her a chance to savour the feeling, he pulled his arms out of her grip and took hold of her throat again. Vix choked as he slammed her back into the glass and stepped closer, digging his thumbs into the hollow of her neck harder than before. Her bladder almost faltered in response to his raw aggression and there was only one way this would end.

She wasn't going to get away.

There was no escape.

This was how she was going to die and she couldn't do anything to stop it.

She was going to die.

She was really going to die by Tiro's hands, surrender her last breath with his attention directly on her.

Oh well. She let go of his arms, one at a time, and let her head fall backwards, squeezing her eyelids together for moment to blot out the pain. *I tried, didn't I? That's enough … right?*

She opened them again, forgetting to turn her face aside. Their eyes met for the first time and her entire personality seemed to ripple against the impact of his deep blue stare, seconds away from shattering like a mirror struck by a self-loathing fist. She heard a phone clattering on the ground and distantly wondered when she had taken it out of her pocket. As red-streaked blackness shrouded her senses, a final thought passed through Vix's mind.

She should have looked into his eyes before. That way, she might have seen past the beautiful soul that everyone else could see.

She might have seen the void that existed beyond it.

Chapter Two: People don't move around after dying

The vibrations of her phone woke her, the dull buzz of grey plastic against pale wood coming from her bedside cabinet. It preceded her alarm and she stirred before the fuzzy recording of Tiro enthusiastically saying "Hi, guys!" began playing on a loop. A bashfully amused smile accompanied her groan, coupled with a dash of the usual guilt. A greeting specially reserved for weekday mornings.

Minutes later, she was blinking lukewarm drops of water off her eyelashes. Trying not to grit her freshly cleaned teeth as she ran a small hairbrush through the short, half-fluffy, half-oily strands of her dark brown hair. Half an hour later, she left the house with her phone in one hand, having almost forgotten it in her room where she had left it charging last night.

Thank god ... The bus ride would be so boring without it.

Seated next to a window on the bus, an Instagram notification distracted her from plugging in her earphones. She tapped her phone screen without thinking and everything actively operating in her body froze simultaneously as he appeared before her.

Tiro.

It was a close up shot, most likely a selfie due to the absence of his left hand. He was crouching down, visible hand hanging in the space between his knees, dressed in dark blue jeans and an unbuttoned, matching denim jacket. Revealing a white sleeveless shirt beneath it and the shadows lingering in the dip of his aesthetic collar bones. A pair of black and white trainers completed the outfit, complemented by a sapphire stud in one ear and a silver chain that dipped out of sight behind the neck of his vest top.

The skies behind him were a glorious blend of blue and gold, presumably the sight he had unsuccessfully tried to draw attention to. The golden gleam in his stare mixed with a darkness cast by the sunlight across his features. Combined with the phantom smile curving his lips and highlighted by a slight head tilt, it was enough to rival the most breath-taking scenic view ever captured in a single photograph.

He had captioned the picture with two simple phrases: Just me under this sky. Just this sky above me.

He's trying to kill me. He knows what I do every day and he's punishing me for it. Vix pressed the back of her hand to her mouth, concealing the tell-tale convulsion of her throat muscles, and had to close her eyes. Biting down on her bottom lip for a few seconds before daring to look at the photo again. *The worst part is ... I don't even mind. Holy crap ...*

He had tried to kill her.

He was killing her.

And she *did* mind.

WHEN HER EYES OPENED again, genuine surprise kick-started her nervous system. Though she moved to sit up at once, Vix only managed to roll off the bed beneath her, landing on her back with a breathless gasp. The memory of that morning was fresh behind her eyes but a white ceiling – ridiculously decorated with plastic glow-in-the-dark stars – filled her sight. The wooden bed frame on her right was half concealed by a black duvet and pillow printed with a pattern of multi-coloured hearts.

Her gasp had been amplified by the space in the room, bouncing off a number of neatly cello-taped cardboard boxes piled up along one wall and a bed side cabinet that was not where it was supposed to be. The soft smell of melted wax and peaches drew attention to the candle placed on top of it.

Why am I here? Layers of duct tape – wrapped around her torso at elbow level – kept her arms bound to her sides. Panic flickered in the background of her thoughts. *Where is here? Where's Ti –*

Somewhere close-by, a door clicked gently as it opened and again as it closed, followed by creaking floorboards.

Crap! Crap! Crap! Vix rolled over onto her side, tucking her knees underneath her. Bracing her forehead against the floor to push her upper body into a less horizontal position. The door of the room opened behind her. *Oh fu –*

"Haha ... I knew you were awake. I sensed it," said the person that had entered the room, his low voice unexpectedly bright considering the shady things she had seen him do.

My legs aren't tied ... Lunging forward, Vix used the closest grey wall for balance and slid along it until she was facing the rest of the room.

Facing Tiro, who set down several brown paper bags with a bizarrely shy smile before looking at her, his head tilted ever so slightly to one side.

"Wah ...You might look like the static, academic type but I've never seen anyone move around so much. Especially after – everything."

*Most people **don't** move around after dying ...*

He chuckled awkwardly. Before, that same laugh would have turned her brain twenty shades of pink. Now, it shrivelled under the memory of his warped smile as he had watched the life bleed out of Rob. "Never judge a book by its cover or what, huh?"

This is Tiro's place. Maybe even his room. This is what his home smells like. She gripped the side of her trousers, noticing her jacket on the floor between them. Displaced from blanketing her body by the vigour of her waking antics. She was acutely aware of its reassuring thickness missing between her fingertips. *He's talking to me. He's looking right at me. I can't ... Oh my god, where are my glasses? I can't –*

"I noticed this earlier but – Most people call for help or beg or – or scream at least, you know?" He stepped forward, picking up her jacket and shaking it out. "You *can* talk, right? You can hear me?"

Vix breathed in shakily, nodding, her eyes averted from his. *Why doesn't he **sound** any different?*

"Oh thank goodness. Because that would've made me feel *really* bad." An odd sincerity coated his voice as he folded her coat, placing it on the end of the bed before gesturing at a space next to it. "Why don't you sit down?"

She cleared her throat and shook her head, listening intently.

"Why not?" He scanned the duvet, pouting a little, fingers tracing the bed frame. "It's clean, I promise. It's a spare bed for guests."

Guests? I'm not his guest. No one else seemed to be in the house. No movement above or below the room they were standing in. No voices through the walls. *We're alone in here. I'm alone with Tiro in his house. But he's a –*

Tiro moved closer, pressing one hand to the wall above her shoulder and waving the other in front of her downcast eyes.

"I don't like talking to myself." Forced humour swelled his voice; a balloon ready to burst and shower her with icy water. "It's lonely."

His fingers were around her neck again, destabilising the rhythm of her lungs, but Vix knew he wasn't actually touching her. Because his perfect, angelic face was a hand-span from her own, his blue eyes wide and hurt, the unnatural smile on his lips tightening his jawline instead of moisturising his stare. The smell of the candle, the room, gave way to the minty toothpaste on his words and the musky sweat beading his hairline.

"I'm sorry," she croaked, her voice a friction burn in the silence between them, turning her face aside until she couldn't taste his breath.

"That ... wasn't what I thought you were going to say," he replied after a moment, his tone coloured by genuine amusement. "Why are *you* sorry? I'm the one who kidnapped you. And chased you. And strangled you. Huh ... I don't like where this is going."

Why does he sound like we're just playing a game or something. Vix swallowed as he rubbed his lower lip with the side of his thumb, keeping as still as possible. *This is real, right? If this was a game, that's exactly how he'd talk about it. But this is crazy. Tiro isn't crazy –*

"Ah!" He snapped his fingers and she jumped, arms straining against the duct tape by reflex. "Is that why you're not talking much? Is your throat still hurting from -?"

He slid explanatory fingers around his own neck. Her gaze followed the frustratingly seductive movement like a lost puppy. Her mind stored the memory away like a hunting wolf, deep within her precious vault of Tiro-related memories. Only now its walls were tainted by something she could never erase.

"Vix." Her chest spasmed in response to the muted rumble of her name wrapped in his voice and he held her stare, the grip of his eyes death-like.

"You ... know my name?" she murmured, white noise bubbling up from her heels.

Is that all he knows? Dread fluttered behind her breast bone, a trapped bird with vicious talons.

"We work together, don't we?" His hand drifted down, scratching absently at the tail of the duct tape around her stomach with one finger. Every pint of water in her body started boiling. "Why wouldn't I know it?"

"Ah – yeah." She attempted to clear the fire in her throat.

"I thought you looked familiar. Spider girl. When I first saw you, I almost thought you were a guy or something." He peeled away some of the tape, tugging it apologetically. "I mean – not a guy. You don't look anything like a man. It's just your –"

He rolled his other hand in the air by his head, a twisted parody of the Queen's wave. "You don't act like other women."

"What do other women act like?" she rasped, able to breath without the threat of his hand upon the wall, close to the side of her face.

What other women act like doesn't matter right now. She barely managed to avoid flinching as he ripped away a length of duct tape, the sound embarrassingly harsh against her ear drums. *Why am I drawing this out? And who's Spider girl?*

"Nothing like you. Like someone in the wrong place at the wrong time," he said mournfully.

There was too much space in the room, more than enough for the cold to overwhelm the blood rushing beneath the surface of her skin. The black tape had contained the heat, had held her psyche together, and her thoughts couldn't walk in a straight line any more.

"Then – Then why didn't –?"

"– I kill you?" he suggested softly, gaze fixed on the movement of his own hand as it tore off another strip with pointed force. "Why do you think?"

"I – I don't know." She shook away the water filling her eyes, her voice box. "I don't know why you didn't. I don't –"

"Do you want to know?" He leant forward, his mouth dangerously near her head. She shivered, eyes half-closing as he spoke again. "I don't like to kill people, Vix. Especially colleagues. It makes things ... too complex."

The words were warm and cold against the shell of her ear. Her stomach was a scrunched up sheet of paper, covered with useless ideas before being tossed aside. This Tiro smiled like the one she knew. Had the same voice, same hair, same clothes.

But this Tiro couldn't have posted cute selfies with random farm animals. This one couldn't have helped the old reception-ist Sharon carry boxes of files up seven flights of stairs, that day the elevator stopped working. He couldn't be the same person that lit up a whole room, that made a joke funny just by laugh-ing at it.

Could he be the same man she had watched over the last several months, in case anyone tried to take advantage of his unlimited kindness? The same guy that had almost exchanged glances with her, earlier that day, when everyone else had been talking about Halloween parties and planning after work drinking sessions. How could that person and the remorseless human that had nearly choked the life from her exist in the same body?

"But that's not why you're still alive, Vix." he continued, reaching around her to unwrap another length of tape. "There's another reason why Rob's dead and you're not. Want to guess what it is?"

I don't want to. Vix bit her lip as her elbows were freed, clasping her hands in front of her. And waiting. *I've got no idea. Why wouldn't you –*

"Go on. Guess. Guess why I didn't do it." Mischief trickled into his tone. "You seem like the smart type. The rare kind that actually keeps quiet instead of flaunting it all over the place. Like a peacock."

He's praising me. Does he want an answer that much?

"Because – uh – because I –" His attention was directly on her face again, though now he was scraping at the tape around her upper arms.

He chased me all the way to work. So it can't be because I didn't do anything to him, like Rob did. His fingernails dug lightly into her flesh as he removed the tape. *Something changed his mind after he caught up. After he grabbed me. What happened? I did what anyone would have done. Was it because I didn't scream, like he said? Is he trying to see if I'm paying attention? Will he kill me if I'm not?*

"It's so funny. I can actually *see* your brain racing," he murmured. Wonder settled like snow on his features, icily resistant to the heat radiating from her body. "Like a car, well past its speed limit."

How can I concentrate on anything when he's talking like that? She gulped as his arms moved around her again, inches from her clothes, cautiously avoiding her back. *No. No distractions. Not now. Think! Why'd he bother bringing me all the way here? He obviously doesn't care about location. He could've just left me like he left – Oh my god, what's he done with Rob? Is Rob's body here too. Is that the answer?*

"Cha! Light bulb moment! You just came to some kind of conclusion." Curiosity breathed life into his eyes as his fingers struggled with the remaining duct tape. "Though I can't really tell what it is. Which is weird. I'm normally pretty good at ... reading people."

"Where's Rob?" She forced the question out between her teeth, silently begging him not to answer it.

"Rob?" He blinked, mildly confused. "Why would you think he's got anything to do with you being here? He's not in the house, if that's what you mean."

Not in the house? So he really did leave him somewhere ...?

"I didn't kill him, you know. I mean –" He verbally back-pedalled, smoothly, swiftly. "– Don't get me wrong. He *is* dead but – well – I'm not really the one who killed him. I only stabbed him."

Nausea writhed in the pits of her stomach.

"That's not the same thing," he said, responding to thoughts that hadn't taken form in her head yet. Speaking slower as if she were from another country. "He was still alive, when I left him. An ambulance could've saved him, if we had called one fast enough. He would've lived. Which means I didn't land the killing blow."

What the hell is he saying? The urge to vomit crawled higher up her food pipe. *Does that make it okay? Not finishing someone off? If that was the case, we'd all be murderers.*

"No offence but your face looks funny." Something that mimicked concern drew his sloping eyebrows together as he leant back, eyeing her thoroughly. "Are you going to be sick?"

If I say yes, maybe he'll let me leave the room. He must have a bathroom somewhere in here. She paused in the midst of shaking her head. *Once I'm out –*

"Oh no," he groaned, abnormally tense. "Please don't be sick. If I smell it, I'll be sick too."

Did he lock the door when he came in? Vix pressed her lips together and closed her eyes tightly without answering. Convincing noises were beyond her acting skills so she settled for breathing hard through her nose. *I didn't see him lock it. Though I wasn't exactly focused on the door at that point.*

"Okay. Okay, wait!" Panic rippled through Tiro's voice. He removed the last of the duct tape, completely freeing her arms. "Should I get a bag? A bucket?"

She pressed a hand to her mouth, despising the smile against her skin. *How can he still sound so adorable, even after killing someone?*

"Ah wait, wait, wait! Not here!" He grabbed her hand, pulling her towards the door. "The bathroom's this way. Hold it in, okay?"

His fingers wound warmly around her own, almost costing her the faint foundation of her plans.

I'm holding hands with Tiro Kaelyn. She whimpered against her palm a little too sincerely. *He's holding my hand ... willingly.*

He yanked open the door and ushered her past him, pressing his fingers to her back. She bit the fleshy underside of her index finger to avoid passing out on the spot. After steering her deftly down a hallway towards another door, he nearly fell over her in his haste to get her through it.

"Just ... knock when you're done, okay?" He pointed at an oddly polished, white toilet bowl in a bathroom that was splashed with colour. "Air fresher is there."

He gestured towards the sink and backed out hurriedly, his skin the same hue as the toilet. She wouldn't have been able to tell the difference if a time bomb were about to go off.

Is he going to listen? He didn't look like he thought I was faking. Would a guy that can't handle vomit listen in on someone else? Vix blinked at her surroundings, hand falling away from her mouth. *Guess I shouldn't take my chances. Not here, not right now.*

Her knees hit the floor beside the toilet with a convincing thud and she coughed, taking advantage of the pain by groaning as convincingly as possible.

How long does it take to stop puking? She rattled the cold toilet seat, gaze wandering over to the window. *That's all the time I have to get out of here. After that – What? What do I do after I get out? Call the police? On Tiro? That shouldn't even be a question right now.*

She ground her fists into her face, eliciting louder moans of discomfort before falling silent and standing up again. Like the bedroom, the overall theme of the bathroom was young and darkly nostalgic. A bright blue toothbrush holder. Light yellow shower curtains. Green and pink bottles of shampoo and conditioner. A shiny wooden cabinet next to a red make up mirror.

Tiro's combs and hair brushes. His clothes are in that hamper over there. Vix pictured him running a short, black hair brush through his silky, equally dark locks. Watched him smile at himself in the mirror before starting to remove his pyjamas ... *No! No! Don't go there. Focus! Focus, Vix! You're not an idiot. Stop acting like one. We don't have time to waste.*

She turned the tap on, smeared spots of colour appearing on her fingers. The watered down red turned her skin pink –

– The street lamp above him decided to stop flickering for a few seconds, illuminating the slight heave of his chest, the victorious quirk of his mouth and the blood spotting the flawless skin of his face and throat. He lifted a hand, smearing red marks across his jaw in an attempt to rub them off before glancing down at his stained fingertips. And then sideways, directly at her –

Vix rubbed her hands frantically, senselessly, on her clothes. Realising too late that blood couldn't be blue and purple.

Paint. It's just paint or something. Tiro's knock struck the inner walls of her skull, vibrated through her bones. She spun around to face the door.

"Are you done?" he called through the wood. "Did you use the spray?"

"Not ... not yet." She pressed her hands against the window pane, peering through the frosted glass, baring her teeth at the small opening positioned at its head.

Even if I break it, who knows how high up we are. He said this was a house but I can't count on that. She moved away from the window, opening the cabinet like an assassin, veiled by the hiss of tap water. *What about in here? He's got skin like an angel. There's got to be a razor blade or something. But even if he does ... am I really going to use it?*

"Five seconds and I'm opening the door," he said, a reluctant warning in his tone.

Five seconds wasn't enough time for anything. Vix fumbled through a plastic basket in the cupboard, faltering over a packet of sanitary towels. *Does he live with a girl?*

"One!"

She gave up on the cabinet, rifling through a small cupboard under the sink instead. *Toilet rolls. Towels. Bleach.* The thought of what bleach would do to his flawless complexion sent it straight back where she had found it. She thumped her thigh mercilessly with one hand. *I'm stupid. Seriously, seriously stupid.*

"Two!"

She glanced at the toilet brush holder, cringed and rapped upon her forehead, waking up her brain with her knuckles.

*Think! Think! How can I stop him without hurting him? How can I do that without **him** hurting **me**?*

"Three! Four!" *Is he giggling out there?*

She spotted a pair of nail-cutters and nail scissors next to each other on the window sill, snatching them up before looking down at her clothes. No pockets in her work shirt. That morning, she had chosen her only pair of trousers without pockets, relying on her coat to stash away her phone and purse.

"Five! I'm coming in ...!" he sang on the other side of the door.

Vix stood with her only escape tools in plain sight, heart hammering helplessly against her eardrums, as Tiro pushed down the door handle.

And stepped into the bathroom.

Chapter Three: Danger and safety

"I can't smell anything," said Tiro, gaze flitting apprehensively towards the toilet, his slender yet rounded nose pressed into his sleeve. "Did you use the spray?"

"Yeah." Vix tried to breathe a little slower and kept her eyes from the window sill. The nail-cutters and scissors – tucked into the cups of her bra – dug into her skin with each heave of her chest.

"I didn't hear it," he said, faintly suspicious.

*Crap, where **is** the spray? Normally I'd look at it before saying anything else to him. He pointed to it before, didn't he?* Her ears started to ring as he stepped towards her, scanning the bathroom before reaching for her. *Please don't notice. Please don't notice. Please don't notice.*

His fingertips closed delicately around the cuff of her sleeve and he moved his other hand away from his face, holding it close to hers instead.

"Do you feel better now?" he asked, his distrust fading to sweet concern.

"Ah, yeah. Much better." She gulped, tried to ignore his fingers that were not quite touching her chin. "Thanks."

"I wish I could look as cool as you." He spoke as if he were making sense. "When I'm sick, I looks all kinds of gross. And let's not even talk about how much of a mess I'd be if I woke up in a stranger's place."

Any stranger would love to have you wake up at their place – Vix inwardly kicked her own backside. *What's wrong with me?*

"But maybe it's because I'm not a stranger to you," he suggested, poking her collar bone through her shirt, softly, soul-shatteringly.

"What?" The nausea that had briefly died down welled up again. *He knows! He knows that I was following him. He knows what I am. Oh god –*

"We're colleagues, remember?" His hand rolled in the air, seeking to unravel her memories. "So maybe that's why you're not freaking out as much as I thought you'd be."

"Oh ... Right." She forced a smile onto her face.

"Or maybe you *are* freaking out and I just can't tell." His hand stopped moving, palm raised to the ceiling, as he shrugged. He looked sideways at her though they were standing face to face. "What did you think I meant?"

"Noth – I don't know." Her nerves wilted under his extended stare before he turned away, tugging on the sleeve still pinched between his fingers.

"Let's go. You probably need water. And food." He didn't look back at her as he spoke. "Do you think you can eat? I can't, after being sick, but everyone's different, right?"

*If I really **had** been sick, I would've had to brush my teeth and swallow mouthwash. Eating would've been the last thing on my mind.* She quickly adjusted the nail-related items nestled in her bra with her free hand. As they left the bathroom, she spotted the front door, mere steps away from the room they were returning to. *If he locks me in there, I might never get back out. Now's my chance to –*

"What kind of things do you like to –?" Vix cut him off, grabbing the hand that was holding her sleeve. She yanked him backwards – as hard as her heart would allow her – and he yelped as she dragged him over her leg, stretched out behind him. "Ah! What –?!"

He was down. She only managed to avoid falling on top of him by planting her feet squarely on the floor, releasing his palm and wrist hastily. The door was seconds away. She darted towards it, unable to tell if it led straight outdoors from its design alone.

We're probably in a flat or something. Where are all of the windows? She slapped her fingers around the door handle, slamming it down and tugging it towards her as fast as she could. *Even if I can't find a way out, I can still bang on someone's door for help.*

The metal handle jarred in her grip; the wooden door restrained by a safety chain she had missed in her haste to get away. She reached for it, pushing the door forward to unlock it easier, faster. Tiro barrelled into her from behind, warm, tall, unforgiving. The wood shuddered beneath their combined weight, closing with a bang instead of a quiet scrape.

"No!" growled Vix, a sob soaking the following words before they left her mouth. His hands sought her wrists relentlessly, brushing her skin. "No! No! No! Let go!"

She pulled her arms out of his reach, tucking them into the safety of her body, over and over again. Until he grasped a handful of her hair and pulled her head back with a frustrated hiss.

"Argh!" By reflex, she struggled to remove his hand as painlessly as possible. He captured one of her arms, using it to pull her around to face him. "Let go of me, you –"

"VIX!" he bellowed, slamming his fist against the wood by her head. Hard enough to break something, the door, her soul. Deafening in combination with his voice.

"Don't …" She flinched violently, holding her free arm up to fend him off. Noticed how uncontrollably it was shaking. "Don't …"

"Listen to me!" he snapped, his eyes a pair of blazing sparklers on Guy Fawke's night. She shrank away from him as far as the door would let her.

This is the Tiro that killed Rob … He's back … Oh god …

"Why did you try to run, huh?" he demanded, thumping the door at the end of each question. "I untied you, didn't I? I let you go to the bathroom, didn't I? I even said I was going to give you food so why? Why? Why?!"

His fist grazed her shoulder, bruising heat through her clothes. It took Vix a second to realise her legs were giving way, gazing up at him, horrified, as she slid downwards. Tiro grabbed her other shoulder, pulling her up and shoving her against the door hard enough to elicit a gasp and shocked tears. Sharp pain radiated from her spine, from the points of his fingers pressed into her flesh. His anger drew all of the oxygen from around her, from within her lungs, and she fumbled for an answer.

"I'm – I'm sorry –"

"Stop that," he snarled, teeth bared, brows slanted dangerously. "I want your reasons, not your apologies."

The sheer violence in his tone made her curse her existence a thousand times over, hesitant to touch anything that could vibrate so strongly with rage.

"Because I – Because –" The words stuck in her throat. She grasped the collar of her shirt, tugging it away from her neck. It didn't help. "I don't – I don't want – to be – to be here."

"Why not?" he demanded, pressing closer as if he couldn't hear properly.

"I don't want to –" She paused mid-sentence, nearly choking on air. "– die. I don't want to get –"

"Killed?" He reared back a little, still holding onto her shoulder and forearm. "You're worried about dying?"

Or worse. She nodded, shifting her eyes from his. Focusing on the fingers clamped around her solid wrist. *I don't want to live with whatever you're planning to do to me.*

"Is that so?" His voice was a cold smile, compared to the heat of his attention. Vix mentally wrapped her arms around all that was irreplaceable within her, squeezing tight. "That's not the impression I got a few hours ago."

"What are you – talking abou –?"

"You want to know why I didn't choke the life out of you? I'll tell you." He slid his fingers up her shoulder, resting them against the side of her throat. She ducked her chin but he had moved faster and it was even harder to breathe. "Its because you want to die."

"Why do you think that –?" She went still as he held a finger to his own lips, swallowing the automatic response to his accusation.

"I told you. Most people scream or beg when someone attacks them." His hand returned to her shoulder. "But you gave up after seconds."

"I didn't – I ran away." She hated the bitter coffee taste of her own admission but spoke it all the same.

"You didn't fight the possibility of dying."

"I – I *did* fight you." *For all **that** was worth.*

"You gave up way too fast for someone who apparently doesn't want to die." The venom receded from his tone. As if conversation soothed him in the same way that action set him off.

"You – You're keeping me alive because I – because you think I want to die?" she murmured, eyes widening to absorb the amount of pure evil.

"Eh, I guess. So – as long as you want to die – you won't be killed by me." He let go of her without warning, arms raised invitingly. "How's that?"

Meaning as soon as he thinks I want to be alive, he'll kill me? She braced herself against the door with one hand, searching his face over the top of her arm. The truth didn't seem to matter to him at that moment. He had stolen the easiest way out of her predicament. *How twisted is that?!*

"Not a mind reader here but I'm pretty sure you're not going to share your opinion." He took hold of her wrist again, firmly, and pulled her back towards their original destination. "Let's eat."

Vix licked her lips, glancing back towards the door until it left her sight. Certain she would never look at it through the same eyes again.

TIRO WAS NOT A GOOD cook.

She kept that thought to herself, chewing on her wounded pride every time he offered her morsel. It tasted like salty scrambled eggs with perfectly toasted pieces of bread. Her hands – bound behind her – were inches above the mattress beneath them. A plate of "dinner" rested on a chair that he had fetched from another room.

"I only managed to make one," he told her, folding the next piece of toast around a bit of egg in preparation. "There's a whole set but I got bored. And the table looks too heavy."

He's got a bipolar issue or something. Tiro was smiling as he spoke, hastily catching a free-falling chunk of egg, dislodged by the enthusiasm of his gestures. As if he hadn't hammered the door – after pinning her to it – less than half an hour ago. *It's got to be something like that. He must have a mental illness so he can't control his ... his temper.*

He couldn't cook well but Tiro seemed to enjoy feeding her, occasionally turning a mouthful of food into an aeroplane. He whined like an aircraft before crash-landing each one onto her tongue.

There's no way I'd let anyone get away with this before. Humiliation seemed to add extra salt to the meal. *Absolutely no way. Why am I letting him treat me like this? Because I don't want to die ... No. Because I don't want him to do anything worse. Not him.*

"Isn't it nice?" he asked. His fingertips brushed against her lips as he popped another morsel in between them and pointed at her face straight afterwards. "Why's your nose all wrinkly like that?"

She shook her head, chewing as enthusiastically as possible. Tiro picked up more egg and toast, eating it himself before licking his fingers. She almost choked, averting her gaze from him to douse the fire in her cheeks.

"Ack!" He clapped a hand to his mouth, almond shaped eyes widening before he sprung to his feet and fled the room. "Water! Water!"

Vix swallowed the last bit of food and acknowledged the desert in her throat with a low groan.

"Why didn't you say anything?" he demanded, walking back into the room with a glass of water. Water traced his chin until he wiped it away with his fist. "Urgh, I feel like I just ate something from the Dead Sea."

He sat down next to her and held the glass out towards her face. Gratitude swelled inside her. She inwardly battered it back down with self-respect.

"Here." He shook his head, contradicting the motion with a victorious grin. "I told you, you want to off yourself. Not under my roof, you hear me? I'll buy a cookbook if I have to."

Vix leant forward slowly, concealing her desperation as she drank. Half-closing her eyes, she tilted her head back in sync with the movement of the glass. Though she expected him to spill water up her nose, he seemed used to the action. Angling the cup unhurriedly, watching the flow of water carefully and predicting the way it would move with ease.

How can a killer know how to care for someone like this? She pursed her lips as he pulled a packet of tissue from his trouser pocket. He proceeded to dab at the moisture around her mouth and chin, folding the tissue over before wiping a new patch of skin. *Even normal peop – even non-murderers sometimes have trouble with looking after other people. Is it because he's more than just a killer?*

"You don't talk much," he remarked, adding casually. "Is that why you take so many pictures instead?"

How does he know –? Tiro replaced the tissue packet and retrieved something else from his pocket.

A mobile phone.

Her mobile phone.

Vix's hands jerked behind her as he tapped her password onto the screen. Tilting his body sideways to turn the phone towards her, scrolling through seemingly endless pictures with his thumb. Hundreds of small Tiro faces met her eyes as they rolled past. *How did he –? No, that doesn't matter. But this ... this means he knows ... everything.*

"It was already open when you dropped it earlier. Then I saw all this and kind of worked out the rest from there," he explained, presumably responding to the confusion on her face. "I thought you called the police while you were running. Like a superhero. Ha ha. Who were you calling anyway?"

"I don't – remember ..."

But she remembered all the different pictures that she had taken, from the moment her entire being started to revolve around his. Photos of him coming to work in the early morning light. His wide shirts untucked until someone cheerfully reminded him. The hair at the back of his head sometimes sticking up until someone that wasn't her either flattened it themselves or pointed it out to him, laughing fondly as they did.

Snaps of him working hard during the day, at a desk that wasn't too far from her own. Taking part in the philosophical debates and multiple discussions, laughing and joking around with his colleagues. Even the ones that didn't have the guts to talk to him first. Even her, though not directly.

Shots of him leaving work with shadows playing across his face and body from top to bottom. At his desk waiting for the last hour to tick by, rubbing his crescent shaped eyes, sleepy but trying not to show it. All the photos she had taken screen-shots of or saved from his various social media outlets.

He had seen them all, collected on her phone, without his permission or his awareness until now.

If I were him, I'd want to kill me right about now too, promise or no promise. Shame dragged her stare down to her knees. She had never been more disgusted with herself. Not even after looking in the mirror. *I never meant to hurt him. Never meant for him to see. But who **does** that to another person? Even if they like that someone. I know – I knew – that it was wrong. I knew it. But I couldn't stop and now – Now there's nothing I can say to make it right.*

"Why were you following me earlier?" he asked, his voice softer than expected. He had already taken enough time to digest the magnitude of her gross habits. "To take more of these?"

|Shaking her head, she remembered the first time she had ever been told off by a teacher. She had done everything she could to avoid being in the same situation again.

"Then why?" A ghost passed through his tone. "Did you and Rob plan to jump me together? Were you going to film what he was doing?"

"No!" The strength of her voice echoed in the following silence. "I'd – I'd never do something like that. Not to you."

"Then you'd do it to someone else?" Now he almost sounded like a parent, gently guiding her to the point where she had gone wrong in life.

"Not to anyone." *But especially not to you.*

"Then tell me … Why were you there? After seeing these, it's hard to believe that it was just a coincidence." His fingers touched the air beneath her chin, drawing her eyes to his as he regarded her from the safety of partially lowered eyelids. "Was it a prank that went horribly, horribly wrong?"

"No, I told you. I was – I was just –" Looking away from him now would be a disastrous mistake, even if she couldn't fully understand why. He kept silent, encouraging her to continue with a nod. The extent of her foolishness reared up, striking her as hard as it could. "I wanted to – make sure you were – safe."

"Safe?" He smiled faintly. "How did you know I was going to be in danger?"

"I didn't," she said quickly, waiting for him to defend his pride. "But – it's Halloween tonight so I thought – I thought someone might try to scare you."

"And instead I ended up scaring you." His fingers retreated from her face and he rubbed away the smirk forming on his own. "So you've never followed me home before tonight?"

Vix opened her mouth. Hesitated.

"So you have." The disappointment on his face wasn't as severe as it should have been. But it still sunk into her chest like a freshly sharpened blade. "Of course you have. And that's why you're here."

"I'm sorry," she murmured, the words sticking to her teeth. Wishing she had the guts to look away. "I'm so sorry. I'll never do it again. I'll leave work, if you want."

"Do you really think you can last long without ever seeing me again?" He raised his eyebrows, as curious as he was confident. "I'm not a stalker. I don't get obsessed with many things. But I'm pretty sure someone like you can't just walk away and forget any of this."

"I – I won't forget but –" His perfect face hung onto her heart with both hands. She could feel it stretching painfully across the distance that she claimed she could put between them. "– but I'll do it. I can do it, okay?"

"You won't go to the police?" He blinked, mouth opening slightly. "You'll leave work? You won't tell the police that you know who stabbed Rob? That you left him bleeding out on a side road because apparently you were that desperate to live? And you'll be fine, living out the rest of your life, knowing all of that?"

She started to nod, stopped and finally managed to tear her gaze away from his as the danger of the moment passed. Replaced now by what the future had in store for her. *As if it isn't hard enough to exist already.* Tiro laughed darkly.

"That face doesn't say you can," he said, running a hand through his hair, black strands gliding between his fingers like oil. "You can't live in public with a secret like that. You'd either have to expose me or – or what? What do we do with you now, hm?"

Does he actually expect me to suggest something? Nothing in the room was giving her answers but she had just escaped the cage of his stare. *He must know that I can't expose him. Not with-*

out exposing myself too. It's not like he'd keep quiet about the photos. Does he think I'd risk it just because what I've done isn't as bad as murder? I'd get less time in jail, sure. But everyone else will know why I was sentenced in the first place.

"Do you have a family, Vix?" he asked, pulling his bottom lip ponderously. "Are you going to be on the news?"

She thought of her parents, in another town. Her brothers and sisters, scattered around not too far from where she lived. The group chat that they used to keep in touch. The one she usually had on mute.

"I do have a family," she confessed. "But I won't be on the news for a while."

Even if you kill me. How long will it take them to realise I'm not busy being introverted but dead instead?

Tiro whistled sympathetically. "That's actually sad. Aren't you close to them?"

"We are close –" She faltered. *Is he trying to find out if he can ransom me for money?* "I'm just – not good at keeping in contact. With people."

"Even your family?" His voice had a knowing lilt.

"Yeah." *You won't get any money out of them. I won't let them pay for my mistakes.*

"So no one'll come looking for you any time soon. Even if you *were* to go missing?"

If he won't kill me, what's he planning to do? Keep me here? Abandon me somewhere? Cut off my tongue and hands? She squeezed her eyes shut. *Don't think about it. Just think about how to get out of this. Do I have a chance? Do I stand a chance against him?*

"You might as well stay here with me then." He stood up, retrieving her plate and glass.

"What? Why?"

He looked down at her and shrugged, smiling sweetly. "Why not? I don't know what to do with you and I can't let you go. What else am I supposed to do?"

"For how long?" *I can't stay here like this. I can't.*

"Wow ... so many questions." He looked away from her, chewing his lower lip. "I guess that's fair. I've got questions too."

Oh god, no.

"We'll stay together until we've satisfied each other's curiosity, I suppose." He nodded decisively, turning back to her. "Until I know enough about you and you know enough about me."

"And – And then what?" Her questions seemed to make him happy.

"And then, my dear, my darling one –" The words had a musical rhythm. "– Who knows? It's the future."

He balanced her glass on the plate, just so he could stroke the top of her head. His thumb trailed across her brow.

"I can't wait until we find out what it's hiding from both of us," he said, laughing tenderly before leaving the room.

Did he just ... decide that I have a future? With him?

Vix let her head sink down until her forehead nearly touched her knees. The phantom of his touch buzzed along her skin.

I hate it ... I hate that it makes me feel alive.

Chapter Four: Trying to hurt

"**B**ed time!" announced Tiro, coming back into the room.

His sleeves were rolled up and his bared arms were damp. For once, they weren't the reason that her stomach started churning.

He's serious. He actually wants to keep me here. Like a guest? No, more like a hostage. One that no one will try to rescue.

"So here's the thing. I could keep you tied up like that." He held out one hand, weighing the pros and the cons. "But then sleeping is going to hurt you. A lot."

He sounds like he knows the feeling. Vix bit the inside of her lip, squinting so her eyes wouldn't widen. *Crap, is that why he's like that?*

"I could just lock this door and hope you'll be good." He extended his other hand, looking down at it critically and then back up at her. "But you've already been naughty today. Can I trust you?"

She kept quiet, waiting for a decision that she had no influence over anyway.

"Or we could do this." He glanced over his shoulder, as if he could see through the wall. "You can sleep in my room and I'll tie you to me. I'm a light sleeper."

No, you're not. She held back that particular proclamation. Now wasn't the best time to tell him that she'd sneaked up on him during an unplanned afternoon nap more than once, right at his desk. Nor how she had marvelled at his baby-soft sleeping expression, taking pictures from as many different angles as possible.

"But then –" His shoulders raised and he rubbed at his nose with the back of a hand. "– Having a woman in my room ... It'll be kind of awkward, right?"

But keeping one prisoner in your home isn't? She blushed, despite her wry thoughts. *I shouldn't be in his room ... In Tiro's bedroom.*

"Ahem. I don't like talking to myself, remember?" he sang.

His voice only made her blush more. *I **knew** he could sing. I knew it!*

"I won't run away," she said. "If you lock the door."

"I don't like people lying to me either," he added, his second statement just as musical as the last. A knife appeared in his hand. He looked it up and down fondly. "There's always a fourth option."

"What – do you mean?" Vix subtly began to pull her wrists apart, against the duct tape binding them.

"I'm no expert but I think there's a tendon, right behind your ankle." He looked down at her feet. She tucked them under the bed. "It's real handy for walking. I wouldn't cut it, of course. That might stop you from moving around on your own two feet ever again. But if I just give each one a little nick –" He flicked the knife gently against the air. "– just a little one, it'll heal eventually, right?"

Does he think I'll just agree with him? A faint ringing crept into her ears.

"That ... You don't have to do that." She shook her head. The tape around her wrists refused to loosen. "Really, you don't. I won't run."

"I was thinking about doing it the normal way. My hammer's in the other room." His eyes rose, focusing on her lower legs. "But what if you get arthritis or something later on, when you're old? Broken bones feel the cold more than usual, I heard. Besides, you've got to be in mood for that kind of thing, you know?"

He mimed smashing something violently and Vix suddenly felt dizzy, leaning forward and hoping she wouldn't slide off the mattress.

Breathe. Breathe. Just keep breathing.

"Was it something I said?" He was at her side in seconds, one hand on her shoulder. "You're not feeling sick again, are you?"

Was it something he sai– Is he serious?

"You can tie my hands in front. And lock the door." She took in a deep, unsteady breath. "Just don't – don't cut me. Or – Or break anything. Please. I won't run."

"It'd hurt at first but I've got lots of paracetamol and ibuprofen –" He gestured generously, arm halting in mid-air as she spoke.

"Please, Tiro." Terror wiped out the awkwardness that would have normally accompanied his name on her lips. "Please don't."

How do you use feminine charms? If I had any, now would be the time to use them. Frustration swept beneath her skin. *Do I cry? Pout? Look him in the eyes? What do I do? Would any of that work on him?*

He lifted his hand away from her shoulder and she could feel him contemplating his next move as he stood next to her. She stayed hunched over, hoping he would forget what she looked like and associate her words with a more pitiful, beautiful face.

"All right," he said at last, pointing at finger gun at her head. "We'll do it your way tonight. I'm trusting you, okay?"

His sapphire eyes were wide, giving her a clear view of his sincerity. Vix's heart clenched as if he were a dear friend laying his life in her hands instead of a psychotic person indirectly threatening her.

"Thank you." *Whoever thought I'd thank someone for **not** crippling me.*

"But if you try anything, I'm going to have to do more than just hurt your feet," he continued. The casual tone of his voice sent her stress levels up like a rocket. "I might have to damage a hand or two, okay? So do us both a favour and be good."

"I will," she said. An instant headache wrapped itself around her forehead.

I'd never let anyone speak to me like this normally. But most people don't promise to harm you with a smile like that.

"Okay. Don't get excited but you'll have to borrow my clothes." He headed for the door, stashing the knife away in a location too fast to identify. "Unless you want to sleep in your work outfit?"

"Uh – I don't mind." She blinked.

I can't get changed in the same house as him! Even if he leaves the room. Oh my god, what if he doesn't leave? Because he'll have to untie my arms and he doesn't really trust me. She wanted to cover her face with her hands. *I mind. I totally mind.*

He left the room, returning several minutes later. One arm was covered with night-shirts, the other with pyjama bottoms.

"I thought you might like darker colours better but I threw in a few bright pieces, just in case," he announced, positioning himself before her like a ridiculously attractive scarecrow. "Take your pick."

"Uh –" Focusing on the clothes that lined his arms instead of the proud sparkle in his eyes was hard. "I don't really – Which one is bigger? And longer?"

"Hmm ..." He scanned his right arm, looking from each shirt to her and back again. "That one there. The navy one. Third to last. I think it's the longest. Might not the biggest but I bet it'll fit you fine."

"Oh, okay. That one then." They looked expectantly at each other until he chuckled and glanced at his left arm.

"I can't move my arms or they'll fall off," he told her. "Then I won't know which one you want."

"Then how –?"

"Can't you just –" He pretended to pick up the shirt nearest to him with his mouth instead of explaining and her stomach flipped over. "– do something like this? Better pick your trousers first though."

Should I tell him it's okay? I don't need to borrow his clothes. But what if he gets angry again? She groaned silently at herself. *I should've told him not to before he went to get them.*

Her gaze fell on the blacks and greys mixed into the array of pyjama bottoms, seeking the baggiest pair.

"That shirt goes nice with this trouser here," he said, nodding at his left arm. "The black one closer to the middle. In between the white and blue."

She stood up slowly, her stomach muscles stretching as they supported the movement in place of her arms. Trying not to fall over, she turned to Tiro without meeting his eyes. Keeping her own on the recommended trousers, she hurriedly bent forward and caught the fabric with her lips. He jolted visibly, a bashful laugh tumbling from him in response to her surprise.

"Hee hee! It tickles." He waited until she dropped the trousers on the bed then laid the rest of them over the back of the chair that they had been using as a makeshift table. He picked out the night shirt that she had agreed to use with his freed hand. "There you go!"

He left the room again, after gathering up his trouser selection carefully, and made a circling motion with his index finger when he returned.

"Turn around. Once you get changed, I'll tie them in front." He dragged the chair away from the bed as she did as she was told, swallowing as he came up behind her.

It had been stressful enough the first time he bound her wrists at her back, after her escape attempt. Now it was embarrassing, his breath light on the back of her neck, lukewarm fingers often brushing her hands and arms.

How do I tell him to get out without losing his trust? I can't change with him in here. I won't do it. But how do I make it sound better?

"You think I'm a bad person, don't you?" he asked.

"I don't know," she murmured, licking her lips, forcing her lungs to work.

"Good answer. Thanks for not lying to me." Her hands were free. He only had to untie her wrists. "You're learning."

Am I supposed to tell him he's welcome? She waited for him to continue.

"But you *do* think that I did something bad, right?"

"... Yeah, I guess."

"Why?" He had that tone.

The one that appeared during the debates he took part in at work. They normally involved human rights, morality and theories about life, including different religions and cultures. From what she could tell, Tiro didn't believe in God but he had referred to the existence of a higher power more than once. Knowing what she knew now, his arguments made both some sense and no sense at all.

"Because – because you – because Rob is dead?"

"He was trying to hurt me," he protested calmly. "It was self-defence."

No one defends themselves like that and looks so happy about it. No one with a healthy psyche, that is.

"You didn't know that he was – what he was going to do." Vix froze as he pulled the last of the duct tape off her arms and spun her around by the shoulders, staring right into her face.

"Would it have been right of me to wait and find out?" he asked quietly, absently running his thumbs over her shoulders. "Forget intelligence. Waiting to see if he was going to do something bad to me ... would that have been a good thing to do? By your standards?"

I wouldn't have done it.

"It's not that – There's nothing wrong with protecting yourself." Her skin reddened under his gaze. She averted her own. "It's just – There's only so far you should go."

"Says who?"

"What?" Her eyes flickered back to his face, reading the challenge in every inch of its beauty.

"Who made up all these detailed rules about how to defend yourself?" He held his hands out to either side with a quizzical shrug. "Who said you're not allowed to kill someone who's trying to kill you? Or worse?"

Or worse? Tiro actually said that. She had to stop her mouth from curling downwards into an impressed reverse smile. *I didn't know he had it in him.*

"You're allowed to be good at defending yourself, aren't you?" His voice lowered, his fingers moving back to her shoulders, twisting the material of her shirt. "Who said you're not allowed to enjoy it?"

Don't say "enjoy it" like that, god damn it!

"I don't make the rules," she replied, her voice steadier than she thought it would be. "I just live by them."

"No, you don't." He gave her a small shake for emphasis. "Not always."

"No one lives by them *all* the time –" He didn't let her finish correcting herself.

"Exactly. I just pick and choose when to go with the flow and when I don't want to, just like everyone else." His hands were in the air again, above shoulder height this time. "What makes what you do and what I do so very different, hm?"

*People don't end up with holes in them when **I** mess up!*

"My – failures – only hurt me." She rubbed her wrists distractedly, the impending chill in the room setting her hair on end. "Nobody else."

"So what I do is bad because people get hurt?" He waited for her to nod, triumph trickling down over his features. "But aren't *you* a person? If you fail and that only hurts you, doesn't it still count as a bad thing?"

"The only person you're allowed to hurt is yourself." She ran her fingernails across the pulse in one wrist, trying to ignore his soft scent.

"Why though?" He pinched her sleeve, above her elbow, rolling the cloth between his fingers. "It's bad to kill yourself, isn't it? So why is it okay to hurt yourself?"

"It's – It's not okay. But if you have to hurt someone, it should only be yourself." He was already shaking his head at her but she persisted. "You belong to no one but yourself. So if you damage yourself, it's like you're only ruining your own property. But if you attack someone else ..."

She trailed off pointedly.

"Now we're supposed to see people as possessions?" He covered his face with a hand. "See? That's why I don't think about it too much. I like to keep it nice and simple. If I feel like it, I do it."

This conversation isn't going anywhere.

"No, you don't," she shot back, trying not to mimic him. "Not always."

"What d'you mean?" He eyed her through his fingers, anger rumbling in the distance of his expression.

"S – Sometimes when you don't want to smile at people, you do." Her throat dried out. "When you don't want to be around them, you stay. I've seen you."

"Of course you have. You're my personal stalker, aren't you?" He smiled painfully.

"No one does ev - everything they want to do all the time. Not even someone like you," she said, silently begging him not to ask for an explanation as she ploughed on, strangling her fingers instead of herself. "So it's not that simple. Nothing's simple. Not life, not rules and definitely not people."

"So ..." he drawled, seeming to consider her words carefully. "What you're saying is ... There's no point arguing about this? Because we're never going to know who's right and who's wrong?"

"N – " She read his stare. *He's giving me a way out of this conversation. I'd be an idiot not to take it.* "– I guess so."

He picked up the pyjama set, holding them out to her. "Time to change?"

"Mm-hm." She took them, arms buzzing painfully from the sudden circulation.

"You don't need to look so worried." He laughed. "I'm not going to watch you change. What in the world do you think I am?"

"Are – Are you going to stay in here?" she asked as he turned around, his hands clasped behind his back.

"Yup. Don't strangle me with my own PJs, okay?" A giggle layered his question.

I can't get changed with a strange guy in the room. He said he won't look but ... he's still a man. She remembered Tiro talking with his male colleagues, blushing and hastily exiting the conversation whenever it began to revolve around women or less innocent topics. *He wouldn't ... would he? He's Tiro. But then I never expected him to kill people either.*

"Are you changing?" he asked without turning his head.

"I – I can't." She crushed the fabric in her hands.

"Why? Oh, should I go over there?" He walked to the door and stood facing it, now several steps away. "How's that?"

"Tiro ..." It was easier to breathe with him at a distance. *It's not enough.*

"What?" He peeked over his shoulder, cautiously. "I said I won't –"

"I know. I know." She wanted to wring the material in her hands but it felt expensive and she didn't have the money to repay him. *Why would I repay a guy who's keeping me here against my will in the first place? Maybe I should wreck his clothes.*

"What? Do you think I'm going to have fun listening or something?" He grinned, bold and shy at the same time. "I'm not like that. I swear."

"Could you – Could you stand outside the door? Just for five minutes?" She held up a hand, displaying the same number of fingers. "I'll hurry."

"I don't know," he said, half-turning towards her with an uneasy scrunch of his nose. "The last time I let you do something alone behind closed doors, you thought it was a good idea to introduce me to the floor and run away."

Vix rubbed the side of her neck viciously, keeping her eyes averted. The clothes hung from her other hand.

"What? Are you sulking?" Bewilderment dripped from his words. The silence went on longer. "If you don't change yourself, I'll have to do it for you."

Her eyes snapped up to his face, liquid panic shooting through her veins, only to find him laughing into his palms.

"I didn't think you'd actually believe me." He waved a hand disarmingly in her direction, the cuff of his unrolled sleeve flapping down over his knuckles. "I told you I'm not like that. But, unless you get changed, you'll have to sleep in your day clothes."

She shrugged, her heart fluttering dizzily in her chest. *Why wouldn't I believe you?*

"That's not good for your skin."

Neither is being kidnapped by a colleague.

"Your skin is –" He refrained from moving towards her, banging his fist against his hip instead of leaving his spot by the door. "– it needs help."

"I – I don't care." She bit her lip. *I totally sound like I do. Damn it ...*

He muffled a smile with the heel of his palm, lovely lashes lowered. "I know you don't. I think that's why I noticed you the first time."

She scrubbed her knuckles across her jawline, using the pain to stay focused. *I'm still me even when I'm in lo – Even when I'm not obsessing over something. I can fight it. I can fight him. Tiro's scary but I can be too. One of the side effects of being unpopular. Or is it the other way around?*

"I want to tell you about the first time I saw you, before tonight." He glanced at his wrist and clapped his hands. "Hurry, hurry! I'm getting tired."

"Y – You might be okay with it," she said quietly. "But I don't get undressed in front of other people. *Or* behind them."

A smile shaped his shocked mouth into a crooked circle. "I'm not okay with it either."

"Then you – should understand, more than anyone." She refused to meet his stare, pretending not to notice the way he was tilting his head to keep their eyes connected.

"Is that why you've been stalking me?" His brows rose higher, half hidden by a stray tuft of hair that had fallen forward. "Because you thought I'd understand you?"

I can't think of anyone who would probably understand me less in the whole world.

"I know I was wrong. We – We're too different." She held the night shirt and pyjama bottoms out to him. His eyes – wide, all absorbing – flickered from his clothes and then back to her face. "Look at us. You're beautiful. I could pass off as the human equivalent of a mongrel. You're good with – good at hanging around with people. I suck at it in a hundred different languages."

"Hey, I don't know where you're going with this –" Another laugh, this one slightly uneasy, bordering on brittle.

"You have the ability to go places in life while I –" She cleared her throat, struggling to keep her barbed words from hitting too close to home. "– I'm stuck here, my time wasted on someone who barely even knew I was here. Pathetic. How can a person be any more pathetic?"

"They could be dead," he suggested earnestly and the urge to smile nearly broke her.

"True." She shrugged again, exaggerating the movement as best as she could. "Maybe I *am* better off dead."

"I told you, didn't I?" He pointed a warning finger at her. "Not in my home."

"You can't keep me here forever. Everyone dies." She looked at him sharply, taking a step in his direction. Inwardly shrieking when he shifted back a pace. "So why are we drawing it out? You're going to kill me eventually, aren't you? Why wait?"

"Are you asking me to kill you?" The angle of his body changed so that he was facing her squarely.

"Would you?" Another step. She dropped his clothes into a pile on the floor, watching the way his eyes followed their descent, the way one side of his face momentarily curled into a ghostly snarl. "If I was?"

"Nope." He stopped before his back hit the door, barely refraining from glancing towards it. "I told you, as long as you want to die, you're not going to be killed by me."

"Oh is that what you're planning then?" She stepped over the clothes, looking him up and down openly enough to make her own cheeks burn despite her efforts to remain composed.

"What?" he demanded, apprehension lifting his shoulders.

"You're going to keep me here – with you – until I'm glad to be alive – until I'm happy." She let all the betrayal that she hadn't realised she was feeling wash through her expressions, her body language. "And that's when it's game over. Because then you'll get bored of me and –"

She mimed slitting her own neck, the action awkward around her hands. *Crap, if I'm actually right about this, I'm screwed.*

"So what if I do?" Tiro raised his chin, looking down his nose at her, all signs of amusement wiped away. "You want to die any way, don't you? I'd just be giving you what you want."

"Only when I don't want it any more," she shot back, her insides vibrating as she stepped forward, uncomfortably close a thousand times over.

Stay strong. If I can't handle this, then it won't be too long before he breaks down too. I just have to out last him. She tried not to grit her teeth. *We might be complete opposites but – to stab someone like that – you've got to be angry about something. Not just in the explosive way. And I **know** anger, I understand it, if nothing else.*

"You're the one who has a problem with that, remember? Not me." His hand twitched towards the pocket of his trousers, his right one.

There you are ...

"You can't make me happy." Holding his gaze burned as much as keeping a baking tray straight out of the oven in her hands. "Does that mean you'll never kill me?"

"You kept pictures of me, Vix." He smiled dryly, mirthlessly. "If those alone could keep you this dedicated – make you this passionate about keeping me 'safe' – then what do you think living with me is going to do to you?"

"Maybe you're over estimating your – yourself." She tried to breathe in deeply without him noticing and immediately regretted it, his scent fresh in her nostrils. *I'm so sorry, Tiro. So sorry to do this.* "Maybe all you'll do is disappoint me."

He tried to keep his face straight but his stare wavered and he fingered the weapon-shaped lump along the side of his trousers with a sudden urgency that she was sure he hadn't noticed. She was so busy keeping an eye on that hand that she didn't anticipate the speed of his other hand as it shot out, catching her by the collar and pulling her face close to his.

"Make sure you tell me if I do disappoint you," he whispered darkly, looking down at her lips and then slowly back up into her eyes. "I'm not as familiar with the feeling as you are."

He let go of her roughly, forcing her to back up before he whirled around and pulled open the door. It closed behind him with a bang that made her jump, even though she had been guiding him towards it.

Did he think that would hurt? She picked up the clothes he had lent her, standing in front of the door in case he decided to come back in. She held the pyjamas to her chest, feeling the material on her skin like rays of sunshine in the middle of winter. The promise of warmth, so close yet so far. *That doesn't hurt me. Not that.*

Chapter Five: Do you like aliens?

Tiro didn't return to the room after she finished changing, tucking the nail-cutters and scissors under the bed – in between the mattress and the wooden planks supporting it – on either end of its frame. Nor did he come back when she started to examine her surroundings, lightly knocking the walls in search of a window covered by plaster, eyeing the candle flame and the rows of cardboard boxes along one side of the room. She switched off the light and retreated to the bed before temptation could take over.

Don't provoke him too much. He can do a lot worse than just kill me.

The hem of his long night-shirt hovered just above her knees and the pyjama trousers fitted her almost like leggings, tight around the muscles of her considerable calves, only slightly loose around the top.

The kind of trousers some people dance in. The material was rich against her body. She tried to ignore how much it smelt like the man she had been watching for months. *I'm wearing his clothes, after eating his food. Now I'm about to sleep in his house. How the heck am I going to sleep here?*

She drew back the duvet. A fitted sheet covered the mattress. Just like the door covered her way out.

I didn't hear him lock it. She covered her eyes with her arm, blocking her view of the exit. *But I said I wouldn't run. More than once. And if he's out there, if he finds out I lied to him before I get away, who knows what he'll do?*

But she did know.

"I don't like people lying to me either," he added, his **second statement just as musical as the last. A knife ap-peared in his hand. He looked it up and down fondly. "There's always a fourth option."**

I can't risk it. Vix climbed onto the bed, sitting up against the headboard and keeping her eyes on the doorway. *Not now. There's no way he's going to trust me again so soon. But if I'm still here, still alive, tomorrow night. Or the night after ...*

She glanced around the almost vacant room before redirecting her attention to the door again. There wasn't a clock on the wall or upon the small set of drawers. Nothing to indicate the time of day or night, aside from the information that he allowed her. She bit her tongue, the frustration stinging as much as her hands, which were still unbound.

I should rest. If I want to outsmart him and escape, I'll need all the recovery time I can get. And I won't get any when he's around. She bunched the pillows up to cushion her head and back, and wrapped the duvet around her. *Sleeping upright probably isn't the best idea. But then maybe sleeping at all isn't wise. I **did** make him angry.*

The memory of his expression right before he left the room played on a loop across the screen of her mind. She had once read that anger stemmed from hurt and had questioned the validity of that statement. Until she saw the expression on Tiro's face as soon as the words left her mouth. His beautiful brows lowered slightly, as if to conceal the sudden shine of pain in his eyes. His lips parted to retaliate further but his throat only moved pointlessly before he fled the room.

If he hadn't brought me here, I wouldn't need to say something like that. I would never have hurt him. I don't want to regret it. Vix breathed in deeply, letting her eyelids stay lowered for a moment longer. *It seems even psychopaths can be sensitive about failure. But who the hell was disappointed by Tiro? Were they blind? Deaf? Or did they find out about his violent side? Wait ... am I disappointed?* She opened her eyes again, confusion furrowing her entire face. *Should that be a question? Of course I am. He's not who I thought he was. He's done one of the worst things possible to another person and it's clearly not the first time. How many people has he killed? Is that important? Would it make any difference to how I feel about him now?*

The adorable man she had secretly fan-girled over for months was the same one who had taken hold of her collar and implied that she was a disappointment. It still hadn't settled in her heart even though her brain had made the connection.

What made him decide to play nice until he really doesn't want to? He said it was self-defence but he clearly doesn't think anything of abducting people and tying them up in his house. She massaged her forehead with one hand, cold again despite the duvet around her. *How many other people has he done this to? And what the hell happened to them? They're obviously not here any more.*

The carpet was black, an opposite of the ceiling. *Is this where he lives? It seems like it but I could be anywhere. What if he's not living in a flat but a huge house? With all these expensive clothes, he could be rich enough to own one. A house with an at-*

tic ... or a basement. She rolled her head back against the pillow, groaning softly. *There's no way I'm going to sleep.*

She couldn't remember if Tiro had ever mentioned anything about his family or owning a business. People wondered why someone with his potential had ended up where he was. Many assumed he was biding his time or maybe working on a big project in secret. Some were cruel enough to suggest that he had someone taking care of him in return for other services. Those people were often outnumbered and rebuked straight away by his fans. Vix hadn't heard many of those comments recently. Everyone in the office loved him and appreciated his presence, even if they couldn't understand it.

This morning, I had no idea I'd be here, like this. No idea that the night would end the way it did. That I'd be worrying about my life instead of my sleeping hours.

The morning had begun with the usual bus journey, adorned by one of Tiro's gorgeous selfies ...

"OH WOW. IS HE A MODEL?" asked the girl sitting next to her, her eyes as wide as her appreciative smile as they stayed fixed on Vix's phone. "Who is that?"

"I don't know," said Vix, covering his username with her thumb and smiling down at the picture warmly. "But he's great, isn't he?"

"He's effin hot," drawled the teenager. "And I've got a boyfriend."

And you've got to deal with Tiro and your hormones at the same time. I almost don't envy you. Vix laughed at her enthusiasm, entertained but sympathetic. *You'd never believe such a beautiful person could be working a dull office job like anyone else. The world is normally more biased than that. Not that I'm complaining. If Tiro was where he should be, I'd have no way of being this close to him. Absolutely no chance.*

"Good looks don't fade just because your eyes are focused on something else." She pointed out, clearing the dreaded 'adult teaching life lessons to ignorant youngster' tone from her throat. "Um – so, basically, hot is hot, no matter who your boyfriend is."

The girl laughed but her attention was glued to the photo. Vix thumbed the screen, scrolling upwards until other uploads showed on her feed. Her companion immediately looked up, smiling awkwardly as if she had just noticed that the person she was talking to was the exact opposite of the one she had been staring at.

"Ha ha. Yeah, true." She coughed mildly into her fist, shifting her sight away from the beauty spot just below the outer corner of Vix's right eye. Away from her plain features and the neglected hour-glass shape of her body, hidden by layers of clothing.

You're probably wondering how old I am. Or if you should change seats. Who wants to sit next to someone that drools over pictures of a hot guy in public? Vix resumed her scrolling, taking time to absorb each photo. *I could be someone's crazy aunt, for all you know. Whatever you think of me, I don't care. In some ways, being a careful kid pays off when you're older. You can thank yourself in the long run for some of the things you chose to avoid. Like talking to questionable strangers.*

The girl moved to another seat at the next bus stop. Vix alighted at her own several stops later, perusing Tiro's Instagram page for pictures she hadn't already 'liked' . She waited until she was mere minutes away from seeing the real deal before looking away from his older photos. The ones where he had a puppy. The selfies that he had taken at the beach. The sleepy pyjama shots posted at night, right before he went to bed. The abstract pictures that normally featured his wide, lithe hands along with his own quotes.

Seriously, why is he staying here with us? He could be anywhere, with a face and brain like that. She climbed two flights of stairs up to the first floor office space, pushing open the door with one hand and heading for her desk. *There's got to be reason he hasn't left the company to be a model or something. How haven't I found it out yet?*

She sat down, drawing all the things that she would need for the day within reach of her hands. Logging onto the computer, she opened several online systems and signed into various accounts that tracked her progress more diligently than she ever could. The digitized clock in the lower right corner of her monitor changed and – though her behaviour stayed the same – her focus shifted to the door she had just come through.

It flew open, caught by a quick, hasty hand before it hit the adjoining wall. Tiro stepped into the office, closing the door softly behind him. Vix bit her lip to trap a loud sigh, discreetly shaking her head at her screen. The young man in question was dressed in a pale blue shirt today and navy smart trousers, his coat slung over one arm. He looked like an office edition of the selfie he had shared on Instagram. The one that had nearly killed her.

"Hi, guys!" he exclaimed, the huskiness of his voice softening its volume.

Even if he was too loud in the morning, I bet everyone would forgive him for it. He's the kind of guy that'd get away with murder, as long as he looked like he regretted it for two seconds. Vix hated the thought of letting a man escape justice purely because he looked too good to arrest. *Am I that shallow? I wasn't shallow before I – before Tiro happened. Have I become pathetic? Or more real? Is there a difference?*

"Morning, Tiro," said Suzie from her desk, closest to the door.

"Hiiii." His voice see-sawed deliberately as he grinned and waved at her. The exaggerated enthusiasm of his movements made her laugh.

"Hey, Tiro," said Veer, peering over the railings of the second floor.

"Hey!" Tiro half-barked the word, moving his hand sharply away from his forehead as though saluting a senior officer.

Kayla, furthest from the door, didn't say anything. They all knew she was waiting for Tiro to lean one hand on her desk, his body tilting sideways until he could look at her face.

"Hi, Kayla," he purred, a smile in his tone as he greeted her.

Vix tried to think of cold things; ice, metal in winter, drinking water after eating mints. Anything to stop the blood rushing to her face.

"Good morning kid," said Kayla, as if she had no interest in the young man standing next to her. Despite the wide smile that nearly showed all of her teeth. "Now get out of here."

Tiro turned to the rest of the room with a laugh, raising both hands like someone on the wrong end of a gun. He made eye contact with everyone in range, regardless of whether they were on his team or not. Vix lowered her gaze as his attention swept her way, silently revelling as she heard her alarm for the third time that morning.

"Hi, guys!" He waved both hands simultaneously, breezily. "Hi!"

A chorus of hellos and mornings bounced back at him as he swiped at his keyboard. Logging in with one hand and pulling his wheeled chair out with the other. He slid into the seat hard enough to make it spin on the spot, zoning in on the computer screen as though a pair of invisible blinkers had settled over the sides of his face. The sunlight vanished from his expression, replaced by a cloud of blank resolve. His eye-brows lowered a little. He had a habit of biting his lip when he really focused on anything, keeping the unfortunate bit of flesh trapped for a few seconds before slowly releasing it. Over and over –

"Did you call back that fussy guy yesterday?" Vix turned to squint at Suzie as innocently as possible, blinking away the image of Tiro's mouth. "Remember? The one who just *had* to talk to Tiro?"

"Ah, yeah," she replied. Trying stay nice to a customer who refused to speak to anyone besides 'that clever guy from before' had been hard.

Obviously, Tiro's voice had had nothing to do with his stubbornness.

"What did he say? Did you pass him over?" asked Suzie. They had an unspoken yet strictly followed rule in the office, ever since a certain young man joined their ranks.

"Of course not. The clever gentleman wasn't available yesterday." He wouldn't have been today either. Nor tomorrow. Nor whenever someone too pushy about talking to him called.

No one seemed to have told Tiro about this rule but Vix suspected he knew of it. He had made jokes about his protection squad more than once and smiled knowingly when everyone suddenly pretended to be clueless. *It's not like he's just a pretty face.*

"Good job." Suzie winked, patting her on the back and returning to her desk.

Did she notice me staring at Tiro? Vix's gaze wandered over to rest on him purely out of habit, staying alert in case he noticed her. *She didn't look like she saw anything. Would she say, if she had? She'd probably just think I'm zoning out as usual.*

Tiro sneezed, explosively, covering his face with both palms and eliciting a round of fondly amused murmurs. His cuffs concealed the base of his hands, the sleeves slightly longer than they were supposed to be. At first, Vix believed he had bought a shirt that was too big for him. Which he had. But there had been nothing accidental about his purchase.

All of his shirts were huge with extended sleeves. Over time, it had become his style. Even the manager didn't bother to remind him that his clothes were supposed to be smart-casual, his shirts tucked into his trousers all the time, and that his ties weren't meant to be worn loose. He seemed more like a boy at school or college instead of a man working as a customer advisor in an office with other adults.

"Bit too early in the day to try scaring everyone, doncha think?" asked Veer, having descended from the second floor to speak to his most recently acquired debate buddy. He subtly tapped the tissue box on Tiro's desk closer to the hand seeking its contents. Tiro thanked him, blowing his nose softly. "Getting some practise in, huh?"

"I don't need to practise," declared Tiro, checking his face for any stray unpleasantness before discarding the used sheet of tissue in a waste paper bin beside his desk.

"If anyone needs to practise, it's you," said Veer, sounding just as confident in his own words.

"Ah, I don't think so." Tiro squeezed one eye shut and wrinkled the right side of his nose. *Oh my days, I want to dip him in tea and eat him. Does he think he looks menacing?* "I'm pretty good at scaring people."

"Yeah? And I enjoy working here." The other man punched him lightly, sarcastically, on the shoulder. "Even Casper is freakier than you could ever be."

"Ha ha, you're so mean." He whined, twisting his seat away from Veer and pouting.

"See? Scary things don't pull gir – baby faces like that." His colleague chuckled triumphantly. "So ... got any plans tonight?"

"The answer is no." His voice was squishy with suppressed hurt. *Is he faking it? Or can Veer really hurt his feelings like that?*

"No plans tonight?" The other advisor wasn't being careful, his voice drawing the attention of most staff members. Those that seemed to be harbouring intentions to steal Tiro later on. *Why is Kayla looking this way too???*

"No, I'm not going to be part of *your* plans tonight." Tiro folded his arms across his chest, kicking at the floor to turn his back on Veer.

He doesn't like horror movies. Or being with groups of loud people in crowded places for too long.

"Don't be like that. I've got an awesome zombie –"

"Lalalalalala – No ears, no hearing – Raaaawr!" Tiro clapped his hands over both his ears, making noises that were mentally unstable enough to draw open looks of entertainment and concern from his colleagues.

"Why're you roaring?" Veer sounded breathless, partially from trying not to laugh and mostly due to frustration after failing to lure his acquaintance into a social trap.

"Because I'm the only monster in this room and it's lonely." The shaking of his shoulders gave away Tiro's silent laughter.

Being the only monster in the room makes him lonely? Joke or not, that kind of stuff is really depressing if you think about it too much. Which I'm definitely going to do tonight.

"That's why I'm telling you –"

The trill of her phone – ringing directly into her ear canals via her headset – cut off the rest of Veer's sentence. Vix composed herself hurriedly, taking a deep breath before

answering the first of many calls that still made her heart pound the moment they began. She looked briefly at the time on her monitor. But before she could work out how long she had until lunch time ...

HER EYES OPENED, GREETED by an unfamiliar ceiling. Again. The fragrance of peaches was stronger than it had been the last time, mixed with the scent of cooling candle wax. Fresh, as though the flame had just been blown out. She rolled sideways, the back of a tousled head halting her attempt to push herself upright.

"You shouldn't sleep like that," said Tiro, his back against side of the bed frame, tone unusually flat. "It'll really hurt your neck. If I hadn't done something about it, you could've fallen off the bed."

Oh god, he touched me while I was sleeping and I had no freakin' idea. She cleared her sleep-clogged throat as soundlessly as possible but he turned his head, not quite meeting her eyes.

"You need to call in sick." He held up her phone. "Otherwise people will start worrying."

"No, they –" She reined in her unnecessary protest as his pretty, naturally pearl-coloured nails turned pale against its screen. "– okay."

I haven't been ill for months. Not since I ... She reached for her mobile cautiously and bit her lip when he held onto it, just as she had expected.

"Only say you're sick. Nothing else." He lifted his eyes to her, vivid blue rimmed by thick ebony lashes. "You don't talk that much anyway."

The memory of their conversation the night before re-emerged.

"I – I don't care." She bit her lip.

He muffled a smile with the heel of his palm, lovely lashes lowered. "I know you don't. I think that's why I noticed you the first time."

She scrubbed her knuckles across her jawline, using the pain to stay focused.

"I want to tell you about the first time I saw you, before tonight." He glanced at his wrist and clapped his hands. "Hurry, hurry! I'm getting tired."

He noticed me before yesterday. But he didn't show it. I can't ask him why because I did exactly the same thing. She refrained from pulling the phone out of his hand. *Only difference is, he kills people while I – I only ...*

"Okay." He let go of the phone after she nodded, covering her mouth to spare him from her morning breath.

She slowly shifted into the same seated position she had been in last night. Tiro turned his head again, breaking eye contact, and she felt a twinge somewhere within her ribs. *He's still upset ... but that's not my problem. Yet.* Dialling the number for her team phone line, she coughed until the post-sleep thickness dispersed from her vocal chords.

"Good morning, Kayla from Bluebird customer advisors here. Can I help you?" Vix hadn't expected the smoky voice on the other end of the line to welcome her so convincingly. Not at this time in the morning, with her kidnapper sitting too close, in a room that wasn't her own.

"Uh –" Caught off guard, she resisted the instant urge to hang up. Tried to deal with the sudden wave of emotion that reared its head and stared into her eyes until they started watering.

"Hello?" Though she hid it well, Kayla wasn't in the mood to deal with a difficult call before her first coffee. As a senior advisor, she had to come to work earlier than everyone else yet leave later than them too.

"Um – It's Vix." Tiro didn't seem to be paying any attention to the call. But his shoulders were tense and he was pulling at the knee of his blue woollen pyjama bottoms repeatedly. *He's probably wishing he told me to put it on loud speaker.*

"Oh hello, Vix. You okay?" Kayla's voice switched from professional to easy acquaintance.

*I am **so** not okay.*

"Y-yeah." Tiro's face tilted in her direction. She coughed deliberately. "Uh actually, I don't think I'll be in today."

"Oh no, really?" Her colleagues concern sounded more sincere than she had expected it to. *Is it because I'm desperate for something **not** crazy?* "What's wrong?"

"I'm ... not feeling well." *Perfectly reasonable for someone who saw a fellow staff member get stabbed to death several hours ago.*

"Good for you. At least now you know you're human like the rest of us." Kayla laughed, clearly relieved that she didn't have to deal with anything more strenuous than an ill colleague. "I'll let Micky know."

Rob won't be coming to work today either. He won't even have the chance to ring in. How long will it be before they start looking for him? Vix heard the end of the conversation approaching in Kayla's tone. *Tiro might not let me call again tomorrow. This might be the last time I use my phone. I don't have to explain the situation to her. All I'd need to say is something to make her question my safety – or show her that I'm not okay. If I do that –*

Tiro chose that moment to turn, resting his arm along the mattress and staring directly at her face. His lips moved, conveying a silent warning, as he mimed putting the phone down.

"Don't do it."

"Thanks, Kayla." The will to defy him vanished in an instant, replaced by the memory of his sadistically pleased expression. She didn't want to be the reason he switched back to that and did something to her that she could never erase.

"I hope you feel better tomorrow." A sympathetic smile accompanied the senior advisor's words.

Vix could almost see her turning towards a sheet of paper on her desk which usually dictated the workload she had for that day. *She's ready to get on with her work. She's got no idea that the person she's talking to is trapped by a colleague.*

"Me too." The back of her eyes felt like they had been dusted with glass splinters.

"Okay, bye now." The pattering of fingers upon a keyboard sounded before Vix could return the good bye.

She hung up, staring at her phone for a moment longer. *Oh my god, I didn't call for help. I didn't even try. All because I – Because I'm just –*

"Thank you," said Tiro, plucking the device from her hands. "For not doing anything stupid. It doesn't suit you anyway."

Half a second before he had moved, she considered holding onto it. But that would have thrown a spanner in the works of her plan to lower his guard. He was still gazing expectantly at her, his cheek pressed against the cushion of his forearm, as he slid the phone back into the pocket of his pyjamas.

"Can I – I need to brush my teeth." Her empty hands were easier to examine when compared to his eyes. "I don't need a toothbrush. I can just – improvise."

"Are you going to use your finger instead?" When she didn't answer, Tiro got up. "I've got spares. You don't have to sacrifice your hygiene here."

"Okay." For a moment, she was sure he would lean forward and demand why she wasn't looking at him.

"Bring your clothes. You might as well change while you're in the bathroom." His tone was unnaturally brusque.

She followed his suggestion, shuffling off the mattress as far as possible from where he stood, gathering up her work clothes slung over the back of the chair he had been using as a table. The trip to the bathroom and back was uneventful. The brand new toothbrush was so pink that she wanted to throw up just from looking at it, certain he had chosen it purely to spite her. Back in the room, she held out his pyjama set but he turned his back on her.

"You'll need them again later. No point taking them back now," he said.

"Oh okay." She put them at the end of the bed, her unoccupied hands clasped.

"I didn't tie them last night." He walked over to the drawers and pulled out a roll of duct tape. "But I have to do it now. So turn around."

Why does he need to do it now?

"Are you going to work?" she asked as she twisted around. Breathing hard through her nose for patience as he wound the tape around her wrists.

"Don't get any ideas," he muttered at once, pulling on the roll harder than he needed to. The swear words running through her mind nearly spilled out of her mouth.

"What are you going to do – about Rob?"

"What about him?" Tiro sounded like her little brother in the hands of a full blown, teenage mood swing. *The stupidly hot guy version of a teenage mood swing ...*

"He's not – He won't go work today." She spoke with care, trying not to ignite his temper while he intended to leave her on her own in the house.

Unfortunately, she was very good at triggering irritation.

"An unfortunate side effect of being dead, I'm afraid," he growled, cutting the end of the duct tape – presumably with his knife – and sticking it across the length of her arm.

One of her routinely unshaven arms. Vix winced in antici-pation of how much it was going to hurt to tear it off later. *Next time I get the chance, I'm going to beat the crap outta you. See if I won't try. Who cares about your gorgeous smile? Nothing lasts forever.*

"How are you going to explain where he is?" He wouldn't have to do that but silence would only keep him on edge. *Exactly where I don't need him to be.*

"Why would I know where he is?" he shot back, the beginnings of a sly smile ghosting his tone. "We're only distant colleagues. Acquaintances, at best."

"But his friends – the ones by the pub – they saw him leave with you." She turned around, the curve of his cheek less imposing than direct eye contact. *Crap, did they see me following him? I don't think so but I can't be sure. What if they start thinking I killed Rob and ran away?*

"They saw him walk away with someone called Kaelyn. Someone who could've been dressed up for Halloween." His gaze seemed to settle comfortably on the corner of her mouth. "Besides, how much of yesterday do you think they'll remember, by the time the police find Rob and start questioning people?"

True. They were probably half drunk by then too. They'll be lucky if they remember anything this morning. I should be safe. From the law, at least.

"What did you do to him?" She had last seen his body on the ground in that secluded side road. Seconds before she had turned tail and ran as if the few things that she actually cared about depended on it.

"You could always try doing something stupid," he said, the dryness of his tone surprising her. "That would be one way of finding out."

He's making empty threats. He's definitely still upset with me. She dragged her eyes upwards to connect solidly with his. A fist fight in the form of a long stare. *He isn't expecting me to apologise for hurting his feelings last night, is he? If so, he's got another thing coming. I won't say sorry. Even if he looks like a puppy that*

I just kicked, mixed with a blood stained soldier gazing soulfully into the distance.

"Even if you'd be doing me a favour?" she asked, struggling to keep a nervous smile from her lips.

Tiro leant forward and she nearly ducked away from him. Her hands jerked behind her as he murmured into her ear, which was already sensitive to his voice.

"I didn't say anything about killing you first."

"Why are you keeping me here?" she demanded, talking louder to avoid melting into a fan-girl puddle. "Why waste your time on me? What's in it for you?"

"Does there have to be something in it for me?" He moved back but only a little, holding her stare with surprising coolness.

"Of course there does." She rolled her fingers into fists and opened them out. Repeating the motion because she couldn't afford to close her eyes.

"Why? Because I kill people?" The murderer in Tiro seemed to smirk at her from behind eyes that were still bleeding after her words the night before.

He just confessed to killing more people. Oh god, why? I wasn't ready ...

"Nooo –" She drew the word out pointedly, panic flickering in her chest. Or perhaps it was disbelief. "– because you're human."

This is the longest I've ever had someone look me straight in the eyes. Normally, they only last a few seconds at best.

"You still think I'm human?" He managed to keep his tone even. But his hands found their way into the pockets of his pyjamas.

Not exactly. I've always felt like you were something more heavenly. Now it just feels like hell has tainted your wings and set fire to your halo.

"Well ... you're not an alien, are you?" She released a wavering puff of air that could have been a chuckle, taking the chance to give her gaze a break from his. "If you are, you're missing a few mouths. And your skin is the wrong colour ..."

"A few mou –?" He fell silent. Vix cringed expectantly. His unbidden giggle made her jump and he shed the mood that had been clinging to him like scales of thunder. "That's your definition of an alien? Multiple mouths and funny coloured skin? No big eyes? No funny shaped heads? No goo?"

"Um – I guess not," she replied, shoulders raised and taut.

His expression settled into its dorky, cute guy mode again, his appreciation for all that was different glittering in the entertained crescents of his eyes.

"Do you like aliens, Vix?" He waited for her to nod, albeit uncertainly. "That's good. I'm sure aliens would like you too."

She had half a second to realise that she was in danger – that there was no escaping it – before he placed his hand on the back of her neck. Drawing her close until all she could see were his eyes.

"Just don't make them angry." His warning was little more than a heated whisper. "Aliens can be really scary when they get angry. Sometimes, they even eat people alive and don't let them die for days. Did you know that?"

Vix exhaled shakily against his face but he didn't seem to feel it.

"I – I know," she assured him, clearing her throat. "I've watched – I know, okay?"

He looked at each of her eyes in turn, as if scanning them for deceit. His warm hand left the nape of her neck.

"Glad to hear it." He backed off, a blithe smile on his face that refused to meet his eyes. She had been wrong. The appreciation in his gaze a few moments ago hadn't been for her. It had been appreciation for what he had been about to do. "I'll see you later, Vix."

He waved at her and locked the door noisily as he left. She waited, straining her ears. She didn't hear the front door open or close. It took her a second to realise how hard she was breathing and she sat down on the single bed, leaning forward and closing her eyes tight.

"Holy crap ..." *Is this what asthma feels like? I'll never over-look people with lung issues ever again.* She shook her head to knock her brain back into place. *Not that I ever over-looked them in the first place.*

She straightened up, eyes shut, hearing focused on the door. There was no telling how stealthy Tiro was. But if he could hide bodies without being caught for as long as he probably had, she wasn't going to underestimate his abilities.

He must be going to work soon. If three of us don't turn up, it's bound to seem a little weird. Maybe not significantly but it's not like he can take time off for however long he plans to keep me here. She gulped quietly, breathing in to give her cells as much oxygen as possible for as long as she could. *I refuse to think about how long that's going to be. Either way, it'll give me a chance to escape. Or at least time to work out **how** to escape.*

Vix flopped onto her side and remembered waking up in the middle of the night. Briefly, listening to the hum of silence, tasting the unfamiliar air. *Was that before he came into the room?*

Did I hear him? And if I did – She frowned *– How the hell did I let myself fall asleep again?*

THE FRONT DOOR OPENED and so did her eyes.

She hadn't quite drifted into unconsciousness but had been pretty damn close to it, her heart rate levelling out comfortably. It spiked in response to the door closing with a bang and Vix sat up, reeling in the semi-darkness caused by the insufficient flow of oxygen to her brain.

When did Tiro go out? Is he leaving for work now? I wish I knew what time it is. I swear I've been on this bed for a thousand years ...

Rushed footsteps in the corridor sent a wave of bile through her stomach and she shifted, facing the bedroom door squarely. As if it were possible to be prepared for anything or anyone that decided to come through it.

What if it's not him? What if it's someone else in his house? A burglar? Or maybe a friend? Vix twisted her wrists, trying to wriggle them out of the duct tape. *What do I do? Just play along? Tell them what's going on?*

She clenched her teeth against a frustrated growl, her mind buzzing.

What the hell am I going to do –?

Chapter Six: The scary tone

In the middle of her hastily patched together thoughts, a key crunched impatiently into the bedroom door lock and turned. Vix had a second to consider rising to her feet.

*If it's not him, I'll take the risk. What're the chances I'll run into **two** mentally unstable people in the space of twenty-four – no, maybe forty-eight hours?*

The door opened, steadied by a hand lined with attractively prominent tendons. Tiro stepped into the room, breathing hard, a white bag hanging from his other hand.

Oh, you've got to be kidding me …

"I made it in time. Yay!" He glanced at his watch and pumped a fist in the air, holding up the bag as though it were a trophy. "I got you some food."

Vix strove to pay attention to what he was saying and do-ing, instead of the sweat shining upon his forehead and lining the sides of his throat. The top three buttons of his work shirt had come undone and she knew that if he came close enough she would smell the salt deposited on his clothes. His ragged voice alone was enough to test her mental stamina. She forced her gaze back up to his face, resisting the impulse to watch a single sweat drop trailing over his collar bones, down into the confines of his shirt.

"Where did you com – Why were you running?" *And why do you look so happy?*

"I had to give you enough time to eat. You didn't have breakfast, right?" He moved towards her. Vix's heart fluttered painfully as he bent over her with his perspiring self and started undoing her bonds. "And you probably need to use the toilet too, right? Before I go back."

*So he really **did** go to work. I was actually alone in here. Why did I sleep instead of trying to get out? Don't I want to escape?* She coughed, moving her head sideways so it wouldn't brush against his stomach. *I can smell him. The ocean ... fruits by the ocean.*

"Argh, it's taking too long. Here, I'll feed you." He dropped to his knees in front of her, fast enough to give her stroke. Placing the bag down beside him, he rifled through its contents. "Do you like Thai food?"

Do you actually care? Don't you remember gripping me up before you left earlier. You were angry. She slowly edged backwards on the mattress, tearing her attention away from the slightly damp hair curling on his forehead. *What stopped him from being angry? Is he faking it again? Is he going to swing that bag at my head? Should I get ready to duck?*

Tiro held up a small rectangle container, showcasing the white rice and crispy chicken pieces clearly visible inside it.

"I looooove this. Tell me if you like it too, okay?" He picked out another one, popping off its lid and lifting it to his face. Pure pleasure rippled across his expression as he closed his eyes and inhaled. "Mmmm ..."

*Is he **trying** to make me a pervert?* Vix shifted uncomfortably, her knees level with his chin. *Who makes noises like that at food?*

"Are you angry with me?" His eyes opened and he lowered the steaming box of Thai food onto his lap. He was breathing easier now, shoulders rising and falling only slightly harder than usual.

"What?"

"You're not talking to me. People normally do that when they're annoyed about something. Or at someone." His gaze rolled down to her chin, momentarily, before returning to her eyes. "Is it about the alien thing?"

The alien thing? The part of her that wasn't trapped in his house laughed inwardly.

"You're the one that – No." She cut herself off. She wouldn't give him the chance to use her words as a reason to get aggressive and touchy-feely again. "I'm not ... angry about that."

"Then what're you angry about?" He stole the thought from her mind. "Because I'm keeping you here? Because I didn't properly explain why?"

She paused before shaking her head, thought about it for a moment longer, and then nodded.

"I thought you'd work it out." He set one of the containers aside, cracking the lid off the other, and placing them side by side. He reached into the bag again, withdrawing twin white plastic forks and a pair of pristine paper napkins. "Isn't it obvious?"

Vix squirmed, her shoulders aching, and realised that she was angry. Angrier than she ever thought she could be at the man in front of her. *I don't deserve this for liking someone.*

"If I let you leave here, you'll go straight to the police, won't you? You'll tell them about me. I can't let you do that." Tiro finally looked up at her again, holding his arms out to either side helplessly. "And I don't want to kill you either. So what else am I supposed to do?"

He doesn't ... want to kill me? She had to bite back a stupid smile, breathing in deeply but silently. *Is he really expecting me to answer that?*

"What would you do? In my place?" *Apparently he is.*

"I wouldn't kill people," she muttered.

"Easy for you to say. You've never had anyone grab you in a deserted alley." He got up and she leant back, eyeing him as he sat down next to her and started cutting away the tape with his seemingly magic knife. The timing of his movements was a little odd. He spoke again before she could pursue the thought. "Or maybe you have and that's why you're like that."

"Like what?" She heard the edge in her own voice and sighed at herself, resigned to years of unlearning her own automatic defensiveness.

"Wah! The scary tone came out." He laughed as if he were nervous. "I mean, you don't really dress up and stuff when you come to work."

"Who dresses up to go to work?" His eyebrows raised as he gestured at himself incredulously. Amusement nearly broke through her walls as she altered her question. "Besides you?"

"Normal people. Women. No!" He held out a finger, correcting himself sternly. "Not just women. Anyone who wants to look good. For themselves or for other people. It's normal, you know?"

"And I'm not?" she asked dryly, grimacing as her hands came free and rolling out her shoulders discreetly.

"Of course you're not!" he exclaimed, scoffing at such a ridiculous idea. "And don't pretend you want to be normal either."

"I'm – I'm not pretending." She turned to him, ready to start a war of words.

But Tiro had picked up a container and was handing it to her with both hands like some kind of Japanese award recipient. He had arranged the fork and the tissue across the top of it, balancing the plastic so neither would fall.

"Good. I hate it when people pretend to be what they're not." He picked up his own as she accepted her meal with tingling hands, pointing his fork at her before her lips could move. "Yes, I know everyone does it to some degree. But that's only for survival purposes. It's a must, if we all want to co-exist. I get that. But don't you think some people go overboard?"

"Well ... yes." She flexed her fingers after setting the tub down on her lap, shuffling sideways so that she was angled towards him. She hadn't expected his body position to mirror hers already. "Some people do."

"Don't you find that *most* people do?" He speared a forkful of his food and blew upon it, lips shaped into a pout that was perfect enough to make any other girl insanely jealous.

Please don't look at me while you're doing that ... Vix coughed awkwardly, glancing away briefly as he began eating. Unable to resist watching his cheeks puff out from the amount of food he tended to eat at once.

"So what if they do?" Fortunately, her voice didn't betray her easily.

"It's ... It's inconvenient. For other people." Tiro dabbed at his mouth with his napkin, capturing a segment of his chicken fillet to chew on. He swallowed it before speaking again. "If people keep walking around, pretending to be more happy, or more friendly, or less angry than they actually are, how can we ever judge what they're really feeling? How can you do it accurately when nothing can be quantified?"

I don't know what's going on any more. She started preparing her food to be eaten as best as her unstable grip would allow. Breaking the chicken up into smaller pieces. Gathering each one onto her fork, with just the right amount of rice, shredded vegetables and sweet Thai sauce. *Is there any point in fighting it? None of this makes sense and I'm tired of hoping that's going to change any time soon. Who cares if I didn't come here by choice? Who cares if Tiro killed someone? Who cares if I don't know where this is heading? Who cares if I'm next?*

"I don't think feelings are there to be quantified –" She felt him staring and bit the inside of her lip. Kept her gaze on what she was doing. "I mean, of course they're not. But why would you want to do that any way?"

"Do what?" He sounded like he was leaning forward, reading her aurally and visually at the same time.

"Why would you want to 'quantify' feelings?" She shook her head. *I hope I'm making more sense than I think I am. Otherwise this is going to get embarrassing.* "What – what's the point?"

"The point is ... you can't calculate something unless it has some kind of quantity." He was quiet for a moment too long and she had to make sure he wasn't eyeballing her with that damn knife in his hand. He had released his fork, the tips of his index and middle fingers pressed against the ball of his thumb. As if he could squeeze his explanation out of them. "So how're you supposed to work out how someone truly feels about you if the quantities aren't right?"

Wow. This got deep really fast.

"You can't calculate how someone – feels about you. You just ... feel back, I guess." Against his eloquence, her words were a one-legged duck standing next to a graceful white swan. A glance at his face, mouth slightly open, confirmed that he couldn't quite appreciate her articulateness either.

"Like I said in the beginning." He straightened up, seeming to realise that she had no intention of providing any clarity. "It's inconvenient."

I kind of agree with him on that one. So why the heck am I arguing? Maybe I just don't want him to start being right about things when I can't get the psycho edition of his face out of my brain.

Vix started eating, parcelling up the food and trying not to burn her mouth. *Everything is uncomfortable enough as it is. No need to make it worse.* Tiro followed her lead, eating in silence. For the first time since yesterday, she felt able to breathe properly. She tried to pay attention to the sound of her own chewing but staying aware of both Tiro and herself at the same time was difficult. *Focusing on Tiro alone is hard enough.*

"You're not disappointing," he said, popping the last bit of chicken into his mouth.

Vix nearly inhaled a mouthful of sweet chilli sauce and rice. *I'm never going to get used to his lack of tact. Or timing. Ever.* She coughed and he glanced in her direction, chewing thoughtfully for several moments before providing some much needed details.

"Last night ... what I said about you being familiar with disappointment. That wasn't very nice of me."

It wasn't even a little bit nice. Did it take you this long to realise that? Or just this long to admit it to **me**? Vix coughed again, into her fist, hiding a painful smile behind it. *Is he apologizing? For this, of all things?*

"I want to say sorry but, if you don't forgive me, I might be tempted to do something horrid to you." He smiled tightly, genuinely, when she cast him a sideways look. Anxiety seeped from her pores. "So I won't say it until I think you'll accept it, okay?"

"Sure," she murmured lightly, shrugging. *What the actual f –*

"Truth is ... I don't think you're a failure." His tone was airy but she could feel his psyche treading carefully around hers. *He's worried about my mental state now? What happened at work? Seriously, I need to know what the hell sparked this off. Maybe then I'll know how long it's going to last.* "But you seem to think that way about yourself."

"What're you basing that on exactly?" She poked around in her rice for chicken and came up empty forked.

"Because you idolised me. At least, that's the impression I got from your phone." He closed his empty container with a sharp snap. Flames billowed up from the base of her mind, responding to the reminder of her invaded privacy. "You thought I was something more than I am. Or maybe something less, I don't know. Depends on how you look at it, you know."

"Why does that mean I think I'm a failure?" She scraped the last grains of rice and vegetables into a corner of the container, bringing the plastic up to her lips to scoop the remaining food carefully into her mouth. Squeezing her eyebrows together to stifle the fury.

"You could do better," he said and she nearly choked for the second time that day.

She put the container down and covered her mouth so she wouldn't spray him with rice. *Now who sounds like they think less of themselves than they should?*

"Do better?" She hadn't intended to sound so doubtful.

Tiro leant forward on one hand, turning her face towards him without laying a finger on her skin. As if he knew how she would move to avoid his touch. The idea made her stomach twist.

"I'm not a great as you think I am. I'm sure you don't need me to point that out to you any more," he said softly. She bit her lip to keep her face from giving away something unforgivable. "My visuals are probably better than most. That comes with its own issues but that's a story for another day."

Vix wanted to ask what today's story was but didn't trust herself to talk. Not with his eyes on the same level as hers and at such close proximity.

"You're great too. In your own way. In a way no one else can copy." He shook his head, gently, as if afraid to disturb the air. "But you focused on me instead. Because I'm more socially acceptable, on the surface. So doesn't that mean you don't trust your own judgement? When it comes to things you should and shouldn't like?"

"I don't care." Indignation reared its head from beneath her lungs, shoving the words out of her chest. "Do I look like I care about what people *think* I should like?"

Who are you looking at, when you talk like that? His eyes widened and she could see herself faintly, swathed in the rich blue of his irises. *Are you looking at me? Or at yourself?*

"I'm just saying that you should value yourself more. That's a compliment." He licked his lips, a flash of pale pink over a duskier shade. "Why're you getting angry?"

Because I've got to pay my rent and you're making me miss a day of work. Because you took my phone and looked through it without permission. Because I don't know who's confidentiality you've made me compromise by doing that and you won't give my phone back. So I have no idea what's going on with the few people I know. The words burned on the tip of her tongue, behind her eyes, deep in her gut. A heat that was acidic instead of fire-like. *I'm angry because I haven't had relaxed me-time since yesterday at lunch and my social battery is about to die. Because that's what happens to introverts when they hang around other people for too long!*

"I'm trying my best to make this easier for you." Tiro's shoulders were taut, his voice a strained appeal. "I could – I could've made this a lot worse for you. If I was anyone else ..."

If it had been anyone else, I wouldn't be here. I wouldn't have cared. Vix pressed her lips together. Felt the pressure of her own teeth. *I only followed because of you. Because it was **you** in danger. That's the problem here, isn't it? None of this would've happened if it wasn't me and you involved. But you're not seeing that as a bad thing, are you?*

"Thank you," she said, throwing the word carefully and watching it knock the air from what he had been about to say.

"Thank you?" He leant back, fingers curling into the duvet beneath them.

"For treating me ... well." *Don't look away. He has to believe me. If I'm right about this, then ...* "You're right. You could make this a lot worse for me, but you're not."

The words were strawberry bubblegum around her teeth, in her throat. Sticky, too sweet, not a flavour she was partial towards. Tiro's wide eyes roved every crevice of her face, narrowing briefly before he turned his head away.

"Are you lying to me?" he asked.

"Should I lie to you?" Vix kept her gaze from straying to his bared neck. "Would that make you feel better?"

"Maybe only for a little while," he confessed and the air warmed in sync with the spread of rose pink across his visible cheek. "But then afterwards, it won't feel good. For me or for you."

"That's what I thought." *Only you can blush while threatening someone.* She took the chance to inhale deeply without being noticed. "It would be ... a stupid thing to do."

"And you're not stupid, are you?" He turned back to her. Certainty stole the question from his stare.

I hope not. She didn't answer, allowing her expression to speak on her behalf. Praying it was significantly more eloquent than she had ever been.

"Okay." He nodded, hesitantly at first. "Thanks for not lying to me."

*Smiling now would definitely make him suspicious. Why? Because it would make **me** suspicious too.* She tilted her head in an angled nod. *He knows I don't want to be here. I'm just thanking him for not beating me up.*

"I should go." He stood up, holding out a hand. After a second, she passed him her empty container. "Don't want to be late for work."

If I make him late, will people notice? She wiped her mouth and wrapped her soiled fork in the tissue. Cringing as he accepted both without a second glance. *I would've noticed. But even if anyone else does, it doesn't mean they'd suspect anything. There's no way they would. It's Tiro.*

"See you later, Vix!" He waved at her, a gorgeous smile illuminating his face like a sunrise. Her stomach fluttered. "Dinner will be even better."

She raised a hand and heard the key turn in the lock before noticing it.

He hadn't tied her arms up. Again.

He's being too relaxed. Is that because I said something nice to him. No, I doubt someone like him is a stranger to kindness. Vix pressed her folded index finger into her lower lip. *Is is because he thinks I'm being sincere? Isn't he used to sincerity?*

It was something that she had always been grateful for. Her personality – reflected as it was in her demeanour – seemed to ward off a good amount of shallow feelings and repel those that were not truly interested in who she was. No one felt the need to impress her or get on her good side because neither would earn them anything that they wanted or craved. Unless they wanted to be heard. Vix knew she had always been good at that. When she could not see, she could listen. Usually, very little escaped the combined forces of her hearing and eyesight. But Tiro had gone undetected.

No. Not completely undetected.

She remembered one afternoon a few weeks ago. The phones had been quiet and everyone had caught up on their work ...

THEY WERE TALKING ABOUT charity events, from what she could tell.

"Look, I get *why* we raise money for poor people and stuff," said Veer, flapping his hands, flustered by his confession. "And why we do charity dinners, projects, that sort of thing. But why do people feel the need to fly out to third world countries and stay there?"

Yeah, I've never understood that either. Vix moved her cursor around on the screen. *I respect people that do it but I'd never do that to myself deliberately.*

"It could be, like, a motivation thing," explained Suzie, perched on the edge of her desk opposite Veer. "It's easy to forget people are suffering when you're sitting at home – or at work."

"Not such an easy task at work," protested Kayla, a senior staff member. Everyone laughed at her bittersweet tone. "Just saying."

Her ears automatically singled out Tiro's voice, his husky giggles clear in the midst of their amusement. He was sitting beside Veer, close enough to accidentally brush shoulders. His gaze flitted from one face to the next, guided by whoever was talking at the time.

"Maybe not at your desk," admitted Suzie, grinning at Kayla. "But you get what I'm saying. Once you've gone to a third world country, it's hard to forget the way of life you've seen there. Especially if you stay for a while. You get to see the pain, the tears, everything they go through up close."

"I can see that on TV though," shot back Veer. "I don't need to sleep in a room with a bunch of people and insects, catch some raging disease and feel hungry enough to die. I can give charity without being exposed to all that."

"Ah, but do you though?" Suzie wagged a cautionary finger at him.

"Well ... There's no need to make this personal." Veer coughed and looked away, igniting a new round of laughter.

"See? There're some things that can only really affect you, trigger your empathy even, once you've directly shared the trauma of someone experiencing it." She raised another finger. "It's not always for motivation. In countries like ours, we can end up forgetting how convenient everything is. And how to appreciate it."

"I've been working here for ten years," interrupted Kayla, scrunching her lips good-naturedly. "Don't you try and convince me that anything is convenient."

"Like I said," continued Suzie and Tiro's smile widened in response. Vix's cursor moved in wild, agitated circles on the screen. "Sometimes we're ungrateful without meaning to be. But that's because we haven't been exposed to how bad it can get."

"I still don't get what's so wrong with using Youtube for that stuff," said Veer, shrugging at Tiro. "There's enough disturbing documentary clips – and other heart breaking stuff – on there."

"You can't smell dirty water and life rotting in the heat on Youtube. You won't wish you had sunscreen or slap away mosquitoes carrying Malaria when you watch this stuff on TV." Suzie persisted with a knowing yet miserable smile. "And I'm pretty sure you'd think twice about wasting your Friday night burger meal, if you could hear kids in third world countries crying because they've been starving for days."

Silence followed on the heels of her words for a few awkward seconds.

"You're right, Suzie," said Tiro in its wake. Though he had pursed his mouth agreeably when Veer looked his way, he had also spent more time nodding in acknowledgement of the other points she made. "For most people, living the life that they dread isn't something they can get over that fast. It's probably one of the strongest memories you can make. Like it or not, pain is easier to remember. Happiness? Not so much."

Suzie nodded, appreciation curling her lips.

"That's some dark stuff you're coming out with, bruh," said Veer, patting him on the arm. "Are you all right?"

Tiro laughed, batting his hand away playfully. He turned back to Suzie and continued.

"But, at the same time, I don't think it's necessary to leave the country to find your 'share' of suffering." He gestured towards the nearest window, his arm moving in a graceful swooping motion. "I'm not just talking about the homeless people here. You know they exist but you don't see many of them. And that's not only because we're here in the office and they're out on the streets."

He paused, giving them time to question him. Or decide that they had no interest in listening to what he had to say. All eyes were on him, as usual, except now they shone with less selfish intent.

"Horrible things happen to people behind closed doors. Enough trauma to flood entire countries confined to a single town." He shook his head, maintaining a faint smile. As if doing so would hold together the light-hearted atmosphere that no one else had broken. *Did anyone else see how hard he swallowed just now?* The faces surrounding him did not answer her. *No? Just me? Okay.* "It's good that people leave to help out poor people in other countries. But when you go so far away, it's impossible to hear the cries for help in our own home, you know? I mean, is it all right for us to disregard the people suffering here, just because those in Africa or other continents seem to have it worse?"

"Are you saying it's not right for us to judge who needs help more?" Suzie frowned, as if considering his words.

"Oh no, no, I wouldn't say that." Tiro raised both hands at once, his full fledged smile returning. "People have the right to do whatever they want, as long as it doesn't cause too much damage. Who am I tell tell them otherwise?" He blew out a puff of self-deprecating air and their team members chuckled quietly, fondly, at his reaction. "People will always judge. It's how we survive, after all. I'm just saying you don't need to leave the country to discover awful experiences. Sometimes, I think gratitude is less about location and more about being actively aware of life around us."

Kayla clapped and suddenly everyone was applauding Tiro's short yet potent speech. *Exactly the way they should be.* Vix followed their lead, moving her hands to the same tempo. Tiro ducked his head with the sweetest grin possible, confusion glowing in his already bright eyes. *If I was in his place, I'd be red as tomato. An organic one.*

"Bruh, if I could spit lines like you, I wouldn't be working here," said Veer, thumping him on the back solemnly. The clapping died down, sparing their absent supervising manager from a formal scolding.

"Ha ha. Where would you work then?" Tiro hid his lower face behind a partially formed fist, his nails most likely pressed to the bashful arc of his lips.

"In higher places. Definitely not here." Veer glanced in the direction of their team leader's empty desk, as though it were a huge spy bug. "That's all I'm saying."

"Higher places? Sounds like you're saying I should die." Tiro looked away, sticking out his bottom lip and grinning as the other man hastened to correct him.

"No, I meant – if you can talk like that, you should be somewhere that makes the most of it. Not in a stuffy office, taking calls." Veer shook him by the shoulder. "Trust me, no sane person would want you in places *that* high."

"Veer, that's so cuuuute!" Suzie's brows lifted, genuinely impressed by his open affection for their male colleague.

"Oh shut up," he groaned. His brown skin didn't conceal the red blooming across his cheeks.

"There's nothing wrong with being cute, Veer," said Tiro, patting the top of his balding head.

"You're the only guy in the world who can get away with saying that."

"Not the only guy in the world," he replied at once. "The only guy in *your* world. Lots of guys out there are fine with being cute or pretty."

"Yeah, but you're the only one that's actually straight." Veer laughed and Suzie told him off half-heartedly.

Tiro turned his head, looking out of the nearest window. It had rained earlier and sunlight shone through the glass, weakened by trailing drops of water. Somehow, the sight seemed to reflect his expression with heart-wrenching accuracy and Vix was sure that she was the only one who noticed it.

"ARE YOU STRAIGHT?"

Vix clapped a hand to her mouth and carefully swallowed a bite of her third dinner with Tiro, wishing she could glare at him.

"Are you?" she asked testily, deflecting before she could think about the implications of her response.

"You're not?" Genuine shock widened his beautiful eyes and froze a French fry on its journey to his throat.

Her heart tumbled down an unexpected staircase in her chest. "... Aren't you?"

He's not ... Why would he ask me something like that? It sounds like a random question but that doesn't mean it is.

"Of course I am." His gaze shifted to the tomato ketchup hat on the French fry. "Isn't it obvious?"

Fire warmed the fingertips of her mind as she handled the topic. One careless question could ruin everything.

"Isn't it obvious for me too?" She poked apart the end of her breaded fish, still crumbling and warm from the oven. *How long before he trusts me with a metal fork?*

"I guess it's not obvious for anyone really," he conceded, eating his chip and reaching for another.

I still can't work out if there's a point to these questions or if he doesn't know appropriate ice-breakers for someone he abducted.

"No. I guess not." She ate another mouthful of fish and chips, sighing inwardly with relief. As long as spices weren't involved, Tiro was good at making home-made meals. His timing was impeccable, as if the ability to burn food was beyond him. He seemed to know exactly when the toast should be popped out and how long to keep a tea bag brewing for maximum taste.

It had been three nights since she had woken up in his home. Today was the first time he had let her sit by the kitchen door as he prepared their dinner, in the small room that adjoined it. The tiny dining room had more character than the room she slept in. Brown sofas and dark wicker storage baskets. A low rise table that looked like it had come from Asia and a sandy coloured canvas depicting a red sun bleeding into vivid blue waves, ringed by trees and bushes with vibrant green leaves.

His kitchen was perfect – all black and steel. A tall fridge-freezer that hummed intimidatingly in one corner and a human-shaped knife holder run through by onyx and silver blades, tilted at an agonised angle. She hadn't seen any stairs yet but the layout of the building was too odd to be a normal flat or maisonette. *Bit by bit, I'll map out the inside. Then the outside. And – once he's relaxed around me – I'll make my move.*

"How old are you, Vix?" His shoulders lifted guiltily. "I wouldn't normally ask a lady her age but ..."

... But I'm not much of a lady? Guess I can't argue with him there. Not convincingly.

"Twenty-nine," she admitted, stuffing a rebellious sheaf of chips into her mouth.

"Only six years older than me then? Interesting." He hummed around a piece of fish. "It's probably old news to you, right?"

She nodded, resigned to occasional reminders of her shameless stalking.

"Are you the oldest in your family?" he asked.

Dissatisfied dark eyes surrounded her. Some looked down at her from a height. Others gazed upwards from below her chin. She nodded again, clearing her throat. Making way for more of Tiro's dinner.

"I knew it. You don't act like a last kid."

"What do last kids act like?"

"Like me." Laughter and triumph danced in his gaze. "What's your family like?"

I don't want to tell him. If he goes looking for them ... She thought of her sister, Keren, powering her way from one job role to the next, climbing ranks with seemingly effortless charisma and compassion. Jivin, her little brother, dancing to-wards fame one shaky step at a time, his personality blazing from each movement, brighter than a thousand suns.

Her thoughts drifted to her other brother, Noah, hopping between countries, video-logging the world and experiencing life to the fullest, spontaneously, remorselessly. And her par-ents, retired after raising four hot-headed children on minimum wage, enjoying the view of green hills and breathing in fresh, sheep-stained air from the closest countryside. *I won't let him get anywhere near them. That's the least I could do.*

"My mum and dad aren't ... together." Vix mushed a morsel of fish in between four French fries, holding the arrangement together carefully. "I've got five brothers. No sisters."

Am I trying to put him on guard? Is that smart?

"Vix." Tiro shook his head. Confusion lifted his eyebrows instead of disappointment. Both emotions put her on edge. "You're talking funny. Are you lying to me?"

"I always talk funny." *You don't have to be so mean about it.* The playfully indignant words stayed in the restraints of her head.

"No, you don't. Not always." He wiped his fingers with some tissue, meticulously, each one in turn. "You don't want to tell me. Why? You think I want to ransom you?"

"You don't seem like a guy who needs money. No offence," she added, holding up an apologetic hand.

"That's observant, not offensive." He smiled, keeping his face angled towards his hands as he looked up at her. The back of her brain quivered. "So you already know I don't need to involve your family in this."

*What **is** this?*

"Then why do you want to know about them?"

"To know more about *you*," he said, scrubbing at his cuticles like someone caressing a pet. "It's not equal ... how much we know about each other. I don't like being disadvantaged like that. Makes me nervous and I'm not so nice when I'm nervous, as you know well enough."

"What ... would you want to know?" The question was deceptively light to her own ears.

"Preferably everything." He inspected his nails. "But we can start off small, if you want."

"I'll – I can't promise to tell you everything." She hesitated. He nodded encouragingly. "But if you keep my family out of it, I'll try."

"That's all I ask of you, Vix." Tiro touched the floor between them with his newly cleaned fingers. *Why are you making this so indecent? With your freaking rich voice and your shiny eyeballs* – "But I'll have to take you up on that offer later. I've got to pop out."

Her non-existent rabbit ears shot upwards. She nodded sedately. "Okay."

Where to? He doesn't leave the house after work. Is he out of food? Maybe it's run out faster because two of us are eating. Should I ask? Is it suspicious that I didn't?

She tentatively stacked the used plates and empty glasses and he took them to the kitchen. He let her wash her hands and use the bathroom. Moments later, he blinked warmly and waved as he left, dressed casually in a T-shirt and loose jeans. So casual that internal sunlight dried out her thoughts and throat alike. She squeezed her eyelids together to keep out embarrassingly inappropriate images.

"See you later, Vix!" He called from outside the room. The front door announced his departure.

Vix was by the first door in seconds, hands raised but not quite touching. She tilted her ear towards its surface. *Did ... did he forget to lock it? I didn't hear the key but then I wasn't exactly paying much attention. Those bloody jeans ...*

Her fingers hovered over the handle, sweaty palms next to cold metal. *He wouldn't relax that fast, right? Just because I said I'd tell him about myself. He wouldn't be that careless. Maybe it* **is** *locked. Even if he's broken his schedule, I can't do anything if I'm still shut in here. Might as well make sure I'm not getting my hopes up for nothing.*

With the inside of her lip pinched between her teeth, Vix pressed the handle down and gave it the smallest tug. The wood slid towards her. The bolt clicked out of its niche in the door frame. An ice age swept over her from head to foot followed by a desert-sized sandstorm.

It opened. The silence vibrated. *The door's open.*

She couldn't pull the handle further. She couldn't let it go. The hands of her inner clock went haywire.

I can get out. I can leave. Now. The voice of caution piped up in her mind. *I need to go now. But what if he comes back? He said pop out. So he won't be away for too long. If I don't go now, I might not last long enough. Not until he slips up again. He might* **never** *make this mistake again.*

Another mindset spoke up, knowing, trying not to tremble. Caution's older sibling, fear. *What if he comes back now and catches me by the door? I might run into him on the way out. Is it worth it? My freedom. Is it worth the risk? I could wait longer, gain his trust. Reduce the risk before making a move. Wouldn't that be better than being caught in the act?*

A previous conversation crossed her mind, a bolt of lightning in the storm.

"Are you lying to me?" he asked.

"Should I lie to you? Would that make you feel better?"

"Maybe only for a little while. But then afterwards, it won't feel good. For me or for you."

Vix stepped back from the door. Held on to the handle. Scrunched the sleeve of her opposite arm in one hand and clenched her fist until she felt her tendons stretch. A knot formed below her ribcage, swelling rapidly. *If he catches me now, I'll lose his trust for good. But if I don't go, I might lose this chance for good. He might be lonely but I've seen what happens to people who cross him. Even people works with. Even people he doesn't hate.*

"That's what I thought. It would be ... a stupid thing to do."

"And you're not stupid, are you?"

I'm not stupid. I can think. She closed her eyes, tightly enough to prompt tears. Her brow ached. *But if I think for too long, he'll come back. Every second I spend thinking is a second I lose to act. Think! Decide! Move!*

"Thanks for not lying to me."

A train of images screeched through the tunnel of her memory. Tiro stepping into the room, breathing hard, triumphantly holding up a white bag. Tiro blowing softly upon a forkful of food. Tiro leaning forward on one hand, turning her face towards him, his eyes level with hers. Tiro scanning her face, wide-eyed, turning away with rosy cheeks. Tiro waving, his smile like the first light of dawn after a long night. Tiro with laughter twirling in his gaze.

He'll be so angry, so disappointed, so sad when he comes back and I'm not here. Vix growled, clenched her sleeve tighter, yelled at her limbs. *No, you idiot. He won't be sad. He won't miss you. That's just wishful thinking. He doesn't care. He only wants to control you. And we're done with that crap.*

She yanked the door open, riding that wave of fury, stiffening in spite of it. The hallway yawned before her, its breath tinted with traces of warm vanilla, clean shoes and cold newspaper. The carpet under her feet was separated from its woodwork by a strip of metal as thin as ruler. As vast as an ocean.

I know where the door is. It's not far. Around the corner. Past the room next to this one. Only a few steps away. Vix shuffled forward, anchored by her grip on the door handle, restrained by it. *I don't need the lights on. I can get there, get out in ten – no, less than that – in five seconds. I can do it. I just have to let go of the door. I have to move. I can do it! If I don't, Tiro wins.*

"Screw that," she muttered, her voice sharp, dizzyingly loud, in the emptiness.

And she left the room, shivering as she plunged into the swimming pool of danger. She stood still, waiting to adjust to the temperature, doubtful water surrounding her will-power. Another soundless step towards the hallway ahead, leading to the bathroom and kitchen. She could almost hear Tiro in the kitchen, humming to himself as he ducked into the freezer and the oven, reaching for snacks on top shelves with tiny grunts of effort. A third step brought her to the corner. She craned her neck, night vision picking up the precise lines of the floor boards, the frames hanging on the walls. The door adjacent to the one she had left behind stood as silent as a sentry. The sensation of being watched fuelled her next step. She turned and the front door was in sight.

Almost there. Her mind convulsed. Her legs moved accordingly. The wood beneath her creaked. *It's right there.*

She passed the door way on her right. Stopped briefly beside the shoe rack. Several pairs were lined up beneath a large mirror fixed to the wall at exactly the right height. *One for every outfit, I bet. Where are my shoes?*

She squinted, bending a little. The darkness obscured important details. *I don't have time for this. He could come back any second. I can walk without them.*

She straightened up, turning towards the front door. Ignoring the voice that asked if she could *run* without them. Her heart tugged her towards the unknown location of her phone. She forced herself to ignore that too. A reflection caught her eye. Not movement. The absence of it. A familiar shape, motionless, leaning sideways in the mirrored doorway. A rectangle of darkness that should have been sealed by a white door.

"You had one job, Vix," said Tiro.

Her hair stood on end, rigid, stinging every inch of her skin.

He didn't leave ...? Her muscles looked into the eyes of Medusa.

"Just one," he continued softly, from the doorway. "I didn't ask you to trust me. I just wanted to trust you. Was it that hard?"

He raised one hand. A screaming mass of words welled up inside her as if he had lifted a weapon.

"I told you not to lie to me."

He switched on the hallway light. The bulb – hanging above her head – was right in front of the mirror. And its illumination left her blind.

"HERE." VIX FLINCHED at the sound of his voice. The corner of the headboard groaned against her back. His bowl in his extended hand was filled with soup. "Eat."

It smelt like a bowl of vomit. Her hands were still shaking from the aftermath of her failed escape plan as she accepted it. Tiro sat down at the end of the bed and ate his soup wordlessly. She lowered the bowl onto her thigh, a slightly more stable platform. Compared to the endless fuzziness consuming her leg and arm, the dull heat of the ceramic was a welcomed distraction. Her stomach tossed and turned like an insomniac and the food wasn't helping. Nothing was helping.

"I said eat." Tiro's low voice rattled her eardrums, shoved searing knives into her soul.

Her chest spasmed, shards of glass in her lungs, a belt around her ribs. She breathed unsteadily, fixing the fingers of her responsive hand around the spoon. It didn't matter if she wanted to throw up. Because she wouldn't. He knew she wouldn't. Not whilst the shattering of glass and the burn of ropes still echoed throughout her body.

She coughed, cowering away from the silence she had disturbed rather than the ache of her voice box. Tiro didn't react, facing the opposite wall. His left shoulder was a resolute fortress, angled towards where she sat slouched. As if he had no intention of acknowledging her presence, except during his 'keep her alive' duties. There would be no more jokes. No reassuring smiles. No considerate gestures. No trace of the Tiro she had known besides the face that he wore.

I did this. If I hadn't tried to get away, this wouldn't have happened. I did this to myself. The soup was salty enough. Vix closed her eyes. It didn't need tears added to the flavour.

The spoon was halfway to her mouth. It was hard to breathe properly without throwing up.

Someone banged on the front door, an explosion in the midst of anxiety.

Vix dropped her spoon. It clattered back into the bowl, splashing hot, orange-red drops across her work clothes. She bit back a whimper.

Someone pounded the door again. Harder. Demanding their attention.

A voice penetrated the coated wood, the dark hallway, the tension between them.

"Open up!"

Gruff. Authoritative. Wildly unexpected.

"It's the police!"

Preview

Vix rubbed greenish, sleep-induced crust from the inner corners of her eyes. Tried not to yawn into her hands too obviously. Last night, she had gone over her allocated hour dedicated to reading webtoons online. She deserved every second of the struggle that she would go through today. Something was ringing. It took her too long dismiss it as tinnitus and realise the noise was coming from her desk phone.

Ugh, I'm not supposed take calls yet. She picked up the hand set, pressing it to her ear. *Though I guess one early phone call won't **kill** me.*

"Good morning. You're through to Vix from Bluebird customer advisors. Can I help you?" The words rolled off her tongue faster – more fluidly – after she had repeated them for a year or so.

Her ability to inject a bright smile into her tone, especially before twelve pm, still needed working on.

"Hello Vix. I'd really appreciate it if you could."

Vix stiffened in her seat, grateful for her lack of expression. The voice on the other end of the line threatened to colour her face like a winter sunset.

*It's that guy they're all talking about. It **has** to be. Holy sh –*

"Can I ask who's calling?" Doubly grateful for her own voice, which was rarely shaken by her feelings, Vix proceeded with the call professionally.

She bit her lip to focus on what the man was saying, reaching up to pull her collar away from her neck. She wasn't sure which was making her feel over heated; the lack of sleep or the images that his voice conjured in her mind. She had to focus on being an advisor, otherwise she'd start picturing tall white candles, illuminating two beautiful bowls of chocolate cake and custard set on a glass table, followed by red rose petals on black satin sheets – *Okaaaay. Not focusing at all.*

"I'm Tiro. I just got transferred here?" Despite the questioning tilt to his words, the stranger with the heated, abyss-like voice vaulted straight into the core of their conversation. "I've been assigned a desk but I don't know if it's the right one. None of the programs I though we'd use are installed. Should I make my own ... profile? I *think* that's what he called it?"

With a voice like that, this guy could look like the bottom of a shoe and no one would think twice about doing anything he asked. Vix blinked at the screen in front of her, fixing the string of pleasant noises she had just heard into an arrangement. One that made sense to mere mortals. *Wow ... So this is how people end up doing stupid things in the name of attraction.*

"That's right. Normally, we create our own profiles. There should be a folder on the desk – or in a drawer – with the details you'll need to get started." She could hear his eyes searching his surroundings, feel his breath in her ear, mildly strained by concentration. "Which room are you in? I could come over and help you set up. If you want."

Only because I don't want to come off as cold. He's new here. No one wants to feel unwelcome, particularly on their first day at a new place. She smiled to herself, eyes half closed as she leant into the ear piece of the phone. Its length cradled her head until she realised what she was doing and bolted up right in denial. *I **am** curious but not like that. Even if he is good-looking, I doubt he'll be my type of good-looking –*

"Well –" He giggled. Her pulse jumped at its spontaneity, its utter lack of awkwardness. "– you won't have to walk too far, I can tell you that."

"Sorry?" *Oh crap, is he in here?* No one else was talking on the phone. Not anyone sitting at the desks surrounding hers. She eased her body language into innocent, relaxed mode. *He must really not look like much –*

"Think outside the box," he suggested, mischief tip-toeing across his tone, its clawed hands raised in nursery monster position. "Or more like, think *above* the box."

A second floor rimmed the room, extending further into the building. Hollow metal rails panelled by polished glass rose to waist height, separated only by the flight of stairs that led to the next floor. It had fewer desks – spaced at wider intervals for minimum interference – and large, padded seats with back rests approved by osteopaths. It was the space normally reserved for team leaders and specialist advisors who did their job better with less distractions. For those who worked harder to earn the freedom and the view.

Tiro was sitting on top of a desk directly opposite her own, swinging his legs back and forth off its edge. He greeted her with a cheeky wave and a gorgeously sincere smile that could have triggered a stroke on its own. Despite the distance between their seats, the awkwardness of the angle, she could see the twinkle in his eyes. As if they had been secret acquaintances for years and had only just had the opportunity to meet face to face.

"Ooooh, that's scary!" he exclaimed, clapping his hands lightly. Making as little noise as possible whilst appreciating what she had done. "It's like you knew exactly where I was before I said anything."

He – How can he sound like the most manly man to ever man and look like ... like ... She tried not to stare at his plain, loose shirt, worn over a pair of cropped grey trousers and beach sandals. *That outfit – Doesn't he know we work in here all day? What about company visitors? He can't walk around dressed like that. And his face – his body ... Not like a woman. Not like a child either. Masculine – definitely masculine – yet different. A newer edition of manly.*

Tiro was lithe, neither tall nor short. His legs were far from stumpy, strong, shaped, elegant. He swung one over the other and tipped his head to one side as she ogled him. It should have looked wrong. His pose should have drawn the wrong sort of attention. Or made people look away uncomfortably. Instead, he seemed like an urban fantasy prince, living on storm clouds. Far above the rules that the rest of humanity felt obliged to follow.

"So –" he murmured softly, turning his head to speak into the extended microphone of his headset. Leaning back on his hands and beckoning her with his stare. "– you coming up?"

Don't Disappoint Me
Volume 2
Coming soon ...

Don't miss out!

Visit the website below and you can sign up to receive emails whenever Sakinah Baksh publishes a new book. There's no charge and no obligation.

https://books2read.com/r/B-A-IAJF-RINZ

BOOKS 2 READ

Connecting independent readers to independent writers.

About the Author

Sakinah Baksh started writing in the heatwaves of Marrakesh, Morocco, after being subjected to book-deprived boredom for several tortuous months. She has not stopped writing ever since, even after returning to England where she was born and raised as the third eldest of nine children. When she is not working at her full time job, Sakinah usually writes dark, emotional, genre-bending stories, enjoys reading webtoons, and watches *anime* or Korean series that mess with her feelings. Her dream is to connect with the world via her stories, make her readers feel a little less lonely than they were before, and be the best introverted author possible.

Read more at https://observingintrovert.wordpress.com/.

Printed in Great Britain
by Amazon

34694875R00071